"Nan, did so[...] you 'Never be all his, [...] forget to hate him, otherwise you'll lose him'?" asked Henry Tudor, king of England.

"I've said it myself," replied the girl.

"And do you say it now?"

"Yes."

"I see. Keep your heart then. I am too old to write desperate love poems to the cold-hearted ~~bitch~~ I love and then tear them up; to pace my room night after night, unable to sleep. I will plead no more. I will not come near you until the day I make you my Queen."

He turned swiftly to leave. Anne Boleyn looked after him and suddenly called out: "Hal!"

He stopped and turned. She ran to him. Falling on her knees, she seized his hand and covered it with kisses. "I do love you, Hal, with all my heart. Take me now. Make love to me. I want to be yours only."

"I have been yours . . . for a long time," he said. And kissing her fiercely he added, "Now for the first time, you are mine, too."

Other Titles in the SIGNET Film Series

Anne
OF THE
THOUSAND DAYS

A Novel by
EDWARD FENTON

Based on the Screenplay by
JOHN HALE and BRIDGET BOLAND

Adaptation by RICHARD SOKOLOVE
From the play by
MAXWELL ANDERSON

A SIGNET BOOK from
NEW AMERICAN LIBRARY
TIMES MIRROR

Published by arrangement with Universal Pictures, Universal City, Calif.; and William Morrow & Co., Inc., 105 Madison Avenue, New York, New York, for the play, *Anne of the Thousand Days*, Copyright 1948, by Maxwell Anderson.

FIFTH PRINTING

SIGNET TRADEMARK REG. U.S. PAT. OFF. AND FOREIGN COUNTRIES
REGISTERED TRADEMARK—MARCA REGISTRADA
HECHO EN CHICAGO, U.S.A.

SIGNET, SIGNET CLASSICS, MENTOR AND PLUME BOOKS
are published by The New American Library, Inc.,
1301 Avenue of the Americas, New York, New York 10019

FIRST PRINTING, APRIL, 1970

PRINTED IN THE UNITED STATES OF AMERICA

HENRY VIII TO ANNE BOLEYN

MY MISTRESS AND MY FRIEND—

My heart and I surrender themselves into your hands and we supplicate to be commended to your good graces, and that by absence your affection may not be diminished to us, for that would be to augment our pain, which would be a great pity, since absence gives enough, and more than I ever thought could be felt. This brings to my mind a fact in astronomy, which is, that the further the poles are from the sun, notwithstanding, the more scorching is the heat. Thus it is with our love: absence has placed distance between us, nevertheless fervour increases, at least on my part. I hope the same from you, assuring you that in my case the anguish of absence is so great that it would be intolerable, were it not for the firm hope I have of your indissoluble affection towards me. In order to remind you of it, and because I cannot in person be in your presence, I send you the thing that comes nearest that is possible—that is to say, my portrait and the whole device which you already know of, set in bracelets, wishing myself in their place when it pleases you. This is the hand of

Your servant and friend,

H. R.

Elizabethan sonnet

Who list to hunt, I know where is an hind
But as for me—alas, I may no more.
The vain travail hath wearied me so sore
I am of them that farthest come behind.
Yet may I by no means my wearied mind
Draw from the deer; but as she flee-eth afore,
Fainting, I follow. I leave off therefore,
Since in a net I seek to hold the wind.

Who list her hunt, I put him out of doubt,
As well as I, may spend his time in vain.
And graven with diamonds in letters plain
There is written her fair neck round about:
Noli me tangere, for Caesar's I am
And wild for to hold, though I seem tame.

Sir Thomas Wyatt (150?–1542)

& Introduced sonnet to England.

One

Over the King's palace at Greenwich darkness hung like a funeral pall. The great stone building stood heavy and forbidding against the wintry sky. In its countless chambers the King's courtiers lay locked in snug sleep. In only one of those narrow windows did a light shine.

It was the window of the King's room.

In that room the fire burned low, flickering to reveal the royal coat of arms hanging behind the bed. The bed itself was empty, its coverings tousled, the splendid spread of cloth-of-gold dragging to the floor. The entire chamber wore, at that hour, an aspect of disturbance and dishevelment. A lone figure sat at the writing table, slumped in the chair. A single candle guttered at his elbow, burnt nearly to its stand. He sat there motionless and brooding, his lips drawn together, his eyes staring emptily ahead of him.

This was the King. This was Henry of England, the giant with a beard of gold and a will of iron, the monarch of whom the ambassador, Falier, had written that "in the eighth Henry God has combined such corporeal and intellectual beauty as not merely to surprise but to astound all men. His face is angelic. . . ."

But the Henry who sat heavily in his chair on that dark, ominous night might have been, almost, another. The gold had worn away. His face was heavy and lined, and his body had already begun to grow gross, encasing in its bloat the youthful vigor and spring that had been the marvel and the adornment of all Europe.

As he sat there, motionless, the darkness in the window panes lightened. The sky was touched with the first streaks of dawn.

Outside, in the courtyard, a horseman came riding in at full gallop. He reined sharply. Grooms ran toward him from the shadows. One seized the horse's bridle; another reached out to assist the rider to dismount, but was shoved aside and sent sprawling as the rider jumped from his horse and strode away toward the King's quarters.

He made his way through the passageways lined with yawning guards. Torches, flaring from wall fittings, cast their uneven light upon his face. It was a face that told nothing. It was a reserved, bureaucratic face: the face of the wool-merchant's son who by dint of hard work, tact, and an uncanny organizing ability had moved far beyond the brilliant and well-born courtiers who surrounded the King, to a position of absolute confidence. And now as he advanced toward Henry's chamber, his steps were quick and businesslike.

The guards threw open the doors of Henry's room.

Far away, across the room, the King rose abruptly in his chair.

And in the doorway, Master Thomas Cromwell pressed his lips together and bowed.

Henry made an impatient gesture with his hand. "What is the verdict?" His voice was a shout. The night had been endless.

Cromwell stepped forward into the gray light.

"Guilty, Your Grace," he said.

Henry's eyes flickered with a last ray of hope.

"All of them?" he asked.

"Guilty!" Cromwell's dry harsh voice replied.

The flicker of hope died.

The door of the King's room slammed shut behind Cromwell. From under his dark cloak, Cromwell drew a packet of papers. He moved toward the table and set them before Henry.

"I have brought the warrants, Your Grace. You must sign them. There is no time to lose."

Henry seized a pen and scratched his name, *Henry R,* across first one, then another.

"And this, Your Grace."

Cromwell handed him a third document. The King scrawled his signature across the foot of it.

"A warrant for the execution of Sir Henry Norris," the King read aloud, "for the high treason of adultery with Anne, Queen of England . . ." His voice faltered. But Cromwell already had placed the next warrant to his hand and had taken the one just signed, sanding it. There was great urgency in every movement Cromwell made.

"—For the execution of Mark Smeaton, musician, for the high treason of adultery with Anne, Queen of England . . ." Henry read dully.

This too he signed. He thrust the warrant aside before Cromwell could take it in hand. Then he took the last warrant from Cromwell's fingers, spread it out on the table, dipped his pen into the ink, and proceeded with the motion of signing.

Then, as he read it, his hand stopped.

"To the Lieutenant Governor of the Tower of London, a warrant for the execution of Anne, Queen of England—"

Cromwell's falcon eye saw the hesitation.

"For adultery and treason," Cromwell said in his harsh dry voice.

Henry's eyes were no longer on the warrant but on Cromwell's pale and clerkly face.

"To be beheaded or burned at the King's pleasure," he said slowly. "Anne. Queen of England. My wife." A long-banked fire sprang to life again in his voice. "My wife, Cromwell."

In the dawn light, Cromwell's features were the color of steel. He said, "She has borne you a useless daughter and a dead son."

Henry's head turned toward the window. "Aye," he said slowly, "when we married, she promised me a son." He rose stiffly and moved his bulk to the window. Through the small panes a touch of green greeted

11

his eyes, surging behind the chill mists of early morning.

In a heavy voice, Henry said, "I must have a son to rule England when I am dead."

At his elbow was Cromwell. "God has always guided the conscience and answered the prayers of the King," Cromwell told him firmly. "He will not let you condemn unjustly."

Henry's face flushed. He turned on Cromwell, biting out his words. "Then why do I hesitate? Is the hesitation from God?" His voice rose, swollen with contempt. "Is He telling me that you are the one who should die, you who found the evidence and arranged the trial?"

Cromwell faced the King. His face was impassive. And he held his ground. "I care only that the King rules absolutely," he replied. "The Queen despised her marriage and indulged her carnal lust." His lips drew together in his bony face.

The mood of the King visibly altered, swinging in a pendulum of doubt over the question of the infidelity of Anne.

"Betrayed me? Did she? Did she, Cromwell?"

Cromwell returned his imploring gaze steadily.

"Your Grace," he replied impassively, "the Queen betrayed you and stands condemned." His fingers pressed down on the paper on the King's desk. "The warrant is before you," he said. His look was unflinching.

Henry spoke, but it was not to Cromwell. It was to the walls he was speaking, or to the rumpled bed, or to the royal coat of arms above it, with the words *Dieu et Mon Droit* embroidered into it in heavy bright gold thread.

"If she betrayed me, she *must* die," he mused, "—if I am to rule and keep my sanity and hold my England off the rocks." He turned his head and regarded Cromwell. "As you say, God will not allow me to condemn unjustly. If I question that, I question my whole life and all that I have done." He paused. "Well, I do question it at times," he admitted. His voice faltered. He shook his head as though trying to muster his troubled thoughts. He stretched his hand out for the quill. "Write it down," he told himself, goading himself with the words. "Write 'Henry Rex' and it's done. I've condemned men, nobles, and peasants—why not a queen?" He let out a bitter laugh. "She's struck down a few herself—or driven me to do it for her."

Cromwell watched, his lips still pressed together. He listened and remained silent.

The King went on, and now it was as though Henry were speaking to himself. "It's only that a woman that you've held in your arms and longed for when she was away, and suffered with her and waited for the outcome of her childbed—no, no!" he broke in angrily on himself. "She promised me an heir!" He stared, red-eyed, at the day that was beating in through the window. "Oh, Anne!" he cried. His voice broke. "Anne!"

Two

Let time roll back to—when was it? Was it only a decade before, or a lifetime before Thomas Cromwell's arrival at dawn with the warrants for the King's hand to sign?

The year was 1526.

And in the banqueting hall at Greenwich that night, there was dancing. In the center of the noble room the courtiers whirled and turned to the high clear tunes that floated down from the musicians' gallery.

Henry watched with a bored eye as he sat beside his

Queen, Katherine of Aragon, daughter of their Most Christian Majesties, Ferdinand and Isabella. In that year, Henry was a man in the prime of his manhood, a robust thirty-five. The blood in his veins still pulsed hotly. Even as they danced, his lords and ladies kept a wary eye upon him, for he was known to be as moody and changeable as the skies in springtime: "A lonely being, a giant in scale, a creature of powerful intellect and insane pride, of cruelty, vengeance and appalling rages, of regal generosity and breadth of understanding. . . ." It was merely simplest wisdom, those dancers knew, to watch one's step in the presence of such a monarch.

Katherine, five years his senior, by then had the appearance of being at least ten years older than Henry. Never a beauty, gaunt and sallow-skinned, from childhood she had accepted her destiny as a figure to be moved about by stronger hands than hers in the endless chess game of Europe's monarchies. Now her dark eyes rested somberly on the scene of gaiety. Behind her, in garments as dark and stiff as her own, stood her ladies-in-waiting and the Spanish ambassador. From time to time her eyes moved, turning to Henry —awaiting his glance and flinching from his indifference—and then turning back to the flashing dancers.

The music was fast now. The dance was a whirling, high-stepping gallop, with two lithe young figures in its center. The girl laughed as she moved. She could have been no more than eighteen, and her partner was that twenty-year-old Northern sprig Harry Percy, heir to the Earl of Northumberland—lanky, unpolished, with a roughness to his manner that made it clear he was not the usual run of courtier. The colors, the music, the dancers, all whirled around, filling the hall with something like the bursting of a garden of spring flowers. And then, suddenly, on an impulse, Percy lifted the girl high in the air and swung around with her. Her laughter rose above the music.

It was the sound of that light, insouciant laughter that made Henry turn his head suddenly. And then, in the same instant that he saw the girl, he wanted her.

14

Katherine's watchful eyes missed nothing that regarded Henry.

"She is new," she remarked, frowning. Katherine had lived at the English court for twenty-five years, but her speech still carried a heavy coloration of Spanish.

"She is Boleyn's younger daughter," Henry said. "She is just back from the French court." He smiled. "Do you like her, Kate? Shall we keep her here at court to cheer you?"

Katherine lowered her heavy eyes. "Whatever you command, my lord."

Henry stared at his wife. Suddenly the Queen's passivity sent him into a rage.

"And suppose I command you to give me a son?" he retorted roughly.

"Would to God I could, Henry," she answered.

"Amen!" he said. "But you cannot, because our marriage is accursed in Heaven and Hell, Madam!"

Katherine rose without a word. Her dark gown rustled as she began her exit the length of the hall, her ladies-in-waiting scuttling along behind her.

And now Henry rose in a fury, his face mottling. He was on the point of ordering her back to his side. But the hall was already in confusion. The music had trailed off into discordance and then silence. The talk and laughter died in the hall. The dancers stood awkwardly. Those in the Queen's path bowed or curtsied.

"Play on!" the King shouted. Henry had recovered himself. "Play on! The Queen wishes it." He smiled grimly. "And I command it!" His hand waved, restoring order to the disrupted gaiety.

The musicians resumed their piping and bowing. The dancers resumed their stances. The revelry began again.

Henry moved off and, whispering behind his hand, gave some instructions to one of the heralds.

Three older men had been standing just inside the doorway, talking among themselves. Two of them were soberly clad: John Fisher, Bishop of Rochester, and Sir Thomas More, the famed lawyer. The third was resplendent in cardinal's red, even to the gloves on his hand, over which a great ring had been placed. This was Thomas, Cardinal Wolsey, the man who had begun his career as the son of a poor and rascally butcher of Ipswich, and whose wealth and power in the realm were second only to the King's.

Wolsey had caught sight of the King. He left More and Fisher and went toward Henry.

The music meanwhile had filled the hall again. Henry was watching Boleyn's daughter. A greedy smile formed itself upon his lips.

The Cardinal bowed. "Ah, Your Grace! If it please you, Sire," he said. His voice was quiet and insinuating, with no trace of abasement in it. It was, in fact, the careful voice of power and authority that knew its strength and was aware, too, of the royal channels through which it must pass to exercise its effectiveness. It was the voice of a prince of the church and of a consummate politician.

Henry glanced at him and his demeanor suddenly became cheerful. "No politics tonight, Wolsey," he called. "No documents. Go and commune with the Devil while I dance!"

"No politics, Your Grace." Wolsey smiled. His fleshy face was rubicund and open. "Only a small domestic matter: a wedding."

"Any man who marries when he can be free," Henry cut in, "is a fool."

Wolsey pointed out Harry Percy and his partner as they swept by in the figure of the dance.

"There is the couple," he said benignly. "Young Percy, Northumberland's son: he is a member of my household. And Anne Boleyn. The parents are agreed and the couple in love. Have they your permission to marry?"

"No," replied Henry shortly.

"I have told him—" Wolsey stopped short. "No? Did Your Grace say—" He blinked in perplexity.

"No," repeated Henry.

"It is a love match," Wolsey reminded him with a smile.

"Then unmatch them, Wolsey," Henry said harshly. "Unmatch them. And send the Boleyns, father, mother, son, and pliant elder daughter, back to that castle of theirs in Kent." Wolsey opened his mouth as though to speak, and then thought better of it. "Send Anne with them," Henry went on. "Send them tonight. Get them away from the court."

"Yes, Your Grace," Wolsey answered dryly.

The King made an abrupt gesture, sweeping his arm toward the ceiling. "I'm bored, Wolsey. I'm bored with the court," he cried, "bored with my Spanish cow. I'm going hunting."

"Hunting, Your Grace?"

Henry nodded. "Hunting, Wolsey, in the beautiful country of Kent," he told him with a shadow of mockery and mischief in his voice.

Youthfully, he strode out in the midst of the dancers. They formed a circle around him, bowing and nodding while the music played softly on. His old friends and courtiers sensed his change of mood. Now, attuned to his joviality, they smiled and nodded, like flowers on whom the sun had decided to shine. Through the crowd Henry made his way, calling out to his various friends as he went. "No ceremony!" he cried. "I have a mind to put you all to shame in a moment." He paused before Sir Francis Weston, tall and urbane, a friend of his boyhood. "You're short of breath, Weston," he declared.

Weston grinned. "A misspent life, Sire."

Henry grinned back at him. "No doubt, no doubt."

And there were William Brereton and Harry Norris, with whom he had cast dice, shot with the bow, hunted, galloped, and hawked. With Brereton he had even compared the verses they enjoyed writing. "Brereton," he called out. "For a poet you keep time like a deaf man."

"Your Grace has learned my secret!" Brereton called back.

And now there was Thomas Howard, Duke of Norfolk, with his shrewd face and unerring nose for which way the scent of power lay. "Ha!" Henry shouted, seeing him there among the younger men. "Norfolk, you should sit before the fire at night at your age."

Norfolk inclined his head. "Better to lie by it, Your Grace," he answered.

"Yes," roared Henry, "but with whom?"

Laughter burst around them at this sally.

Henry moved on. Now he had reached Harry Percy and Boleyn's daughter. His eyes narrowed. "And you, Percy, have feet of lead. You are a Northern clodhopper." Henry smiled. "With your permission," he said, reaching out to take Anne Boleyn's hand. "Mistress Anne, will you teach the King how they dance in the court of France?"

The girl curtsied deeply. Then, in a light steady voice she said, "There is nothing that France can teach England, Sire." Her eyes looked unflinching into his.

"Well said, well said," Henry chuckled. "Are you ready?"

He held his arm out to her. The musicians struck up a new air and the dance began.

The Boleyns crowded forward to watch. Anne's mother and father looked at one another questioningly, and then at Mary, Anne's older sister. Mary pressed her lips together, choking back her anger. Among the onlookers in the crowd stood Thomas Cromwell, lean and thin-faced, in sober clothes. Wolsey left Sir Thomas More and Bishop Fisher with whom he had been standing on the sidelines and came up to him.

"Cromwell," the Cardinal said.

Cromwell turned to him. "My lord."

"Tell Boleyn I wish to speak to him privately," the Cardinal said.

"Yes, my lord."

"And then," Wolsey added quietly, "prepare for a journey."

Cromwell's eyebrows raised almost imperceptibly. "A journey?"

Wolsey nodded. "To Hever Castle, in Kent." He lowered his voice. "For where the dove is, the hawk is not too far behind."

The look that they exchanged was one of complete understanding and complicity.

In the musicians' gallery the gay piping music went on. And in the midst of his courtiers, Henry led the dance with the Lady Anne Boleyn, who had only lately returned from the court of France.

Three

The skies were the skies of springtime, filled with soaring, singing birds. Over the green hills of Kent the King's hunting party came streaming in a brave array of color: cloth-of-gold, velvet, and waving plumes. Norfolk was in the King's party, and Norris and Weston; Mark Smeaton the singer and Brereton the poet were also among the courtiers that rode with Henry that day. Behind them came the soldiers of his bodyguard, the huntsmen, the hounds sniffing expectantly at the ends of their leashes. Across the open country the bright procession bounded.

On the royal wrist rode a splendid hawk.

"Up and after her, boy. Get her, boy!" the King cried.

He flew the falcon. Its wings cut against the sky where a bird hung, singing.

The falcon swooped.

Then the sharp talons struck, and the singing ceased.

"Got her, by God," the King shouted, carefree and triumphant as a boy. "On to Hever!" he called as he put spurs to his horse and rode across the fields in a breakneck gallop.

The hunting party streamed brightly behind him.

Four

In the library at Hever Castle, Boleyn sat writing at a small table.

Sir Thomas Boleyn, ever assiduous, was a man with the cold face of a climber. Under his massive nose lay a weak mouth that even had a touch of meanness to it. Carefully barbered, dapper and stylish in dress, he was smooth and hard. He had made his way from the merchant class to a union with the powerful family of the Howards: his wife, Elizabeth, was the sister of the Duke of Norfolk. And now, with Henry having shown interest in his daughter Anne after a long period during which her sister Mary had been an open favorite, Boleyn knew that further grace and favor were in the offing.

Mary was there in the room with him, her eyes swollen and her lips bitter with chagrin. Her father raised his hands to still her protesting voice.

"Mary," he told her firmly, "it must be said that the King wishes to see me alone."

"He asked not to see me?" she flared back.

He did not look into her eyes. "Not directly," he said.

"That could mean he's finished with me. Has he? Tell me the truth!"

However much Thomas Boleyn might ache for the unfortunate Mary, he was only too aware in which direction the path of fortune lay. "One never gets used to these things," he told her softly. "There's always a hell to go through. But when a girl gives herself so completely—"

Mary flushed. "You know why I gave myself to the King!" she cried. "Since I opened my bedroom door to the King you have lived well by it. Steward of Tunbridge and Penshurst, Sheriff of Bradsted, Viscount, and now King's Treasurer." Her lips curled in scorn. "You don't want to lose any of these revenues, do you, Father?"

Boleyn stared at her thoughtfully, remaining silent for a long moment before he finally replied. "Mary, I've always loved you," he told her. "And all those things are true. The King was generous with me because you were generous with him." He thought, as he looked at her, how quickly her bloom had gone. She looked peaked and too thin: a tired cat where there had been so recently a silken sleek kitten. "But you're a fool," he said sharply, "because you gave him everything and asked for nothing. What Henry is denied he goes half-mad to obtain. And what he gets freely he despises." His look changed to one almost of contempt. "You've lost him. I can't help you. Go now, and cause no trouble. I'll not have you put the rest of us at risk."

Mary's eyes were dull with suffering as they met her father's.

"Go!" he repeated.

The tears brimming in her eyes now overflooded onto her cheeks. Blindly fleeing from the room, she ran into George Boleyn, her brother, younger than she by two years.

His strong hands seized her by the arms.

"What ails you?" he asked, laughing.

"Ask our beloved father," she hurled back at him as she wrenched herself from his grasp and hurried out of the room.

George looked down at Boleyn, who had resumed writing.

"Father," he said," the Lord Cardinal is here."

Mary, meanwhile, hurrying down the staircase, nearly ran into the scarlet bulk of Wolsey. She looked at him with hatred. He inclined his head ironically, but she did not return his gesture of greeting. She cut him dead and continued her blind flight.

Thomas Boleyn made his appearance at the top of the staircase.

"I see you've told the lady," Wolsey said.

A door slammed behind Mary.

"Yes, my lord," Boleyn replied.

Wolsey nodded. "And Anne?"

"No," Boleyn said.

"Why not?" The Cardinal spoke sharply. "The King is almost here."

"Like you," Boleyn said, "I encouraged Anne with Percy. It never entered my head that the King would look at her." For once, even Boleyn, the smoothest of courtiers, seemed at a loss. "What am I to say?"

And now Cromwell, the small attorney, inconspicuous as always in his discreet clothes, joined them.

"My lord," he announced, "the King is here."

"Leave the girl to me," Wolsey instructed Boleyn. "Go and greet the King. Tell him what rubbish you please, but give me time to deal with her."

"What about young Percy?" Boleyn asked.

"Young Percy will do as I bid him," replied the Cardinal.

Outside, a trumpet sounded.

The trumpeter stood on the land side of Hever Castle's drawbridge. And now, the King and his entourage streamed across the bridge and into the castle. Into the courtyard the horses in their bright caparisons swirled and circled. The King's party remained mounted as servants ran from the castle and passed among them, holding up trays with goblets of steaming punch. Henry, magnificent and full of high spirits, waited in the center of the milling scene. Around him pressed the grooms and huntsmen. The air was sharp with the scent of the sweating horses and noisy with the high baying of the hounds.

Into the crowded scene walked Thomas Boleyn. As he approached, Henry was draining his goblet. He tossed it to a servant and leaped down from the saddle with a youthful bound.

22

Boleyn knelt.

"Well, Thomas!" Henry said bluffly.

"Your Grace," Boleyn said, still on his knees.

"It's only your King, Thomas," Henry told him. "No ceremony. It's only your Henry." Nevertheless, Henry held a hand out to be kissed.

"This is a great honor," Thomas Boleyn murmured.

Henry's eyes, however, were already straying upward toward the windows.

Where was Anne? he was wondering. Which was her bedroom? Where was the bird he had come hawking after?

Five

Anne was indeed in her bedroom and aware of the King's arrival. From her window she had heard the trumpeting, the hoofbeats and the voices, and seen the royal procession fill the courtyard of her father's house to bursting.

There was a knock on her door.

"Mistress Anne!"

It was one of the maids bearing a note for her. One glance at it was enough to tell her that it was from Harry Percy. She tore it open and raked it with her eyes. Then she threw it down and sped from the room. She was about to race down the corridor when she caught sight of her mother coming in her direction, gowned to receive the King. Before Lady Elizabeth could glimpse her, Anne turned about and ran in the other direction, disappearing down the far end of the corridor.

Lady Elizabeth entered Anne's room and was surprised not to find her there. She went to the window and glanced out. There was no sign of the girl. Turning, she caught sight of the note lying on the bed where it had been tossed. She picked it up and read it. In fact, she read it for a second time before she hurried from the room with it still in her hand.

Cromwell, with his bland attorney's face, was waiting just outside the door.

"Where is Anne, Lady Elizabeth?" he asked.

Elizabeth Boleyn put the note into his hand. "I found this in her room," she told him.

Cromwell read it hastily. When he spoke there was a note of relish in his dry voice. "It would not surprise me," he said, "if this gave my lord Cardinal a seizure! Shall we find out, Madam?"

Without waiting for her to reply, he moved off with it down the corridor, down the great stairs and into the hall, to find Wolsey.

In the great hall there was tumult and confusion and feasting. The tables were crowded with courtiers who reached out to seize meat from the trays borne by the servants. Other servants handed around mugs of wine. Through the crush of people, Henry moved across the hall to confront his scarlet-robed minister, with a chicken leg in one royal hand and a wine goblet in the other.

"And how is the vicar of Hell this chilly morning?" the King asked the Cardinal.

Wolsey greeted his master with a bow. "Warm enough, Your Grace," he responded. "To be ever busy on the King's business generates a certain heat."

"Ha!" roared Henry. "With your feet on the Devil's fender and your buttocks toasting at God's altar—I'm not surprised!" Chuckling at his own sally, he moved over to Boleyn. "Has he spoken to you, Thomas?"

"He has, Your Grace," Boleyn answered silkily.

"Good," Henry said. In an impulse of friendliness, he flung an arm around Boleyn's shoulders and started to walk him away. As he did so, Cromwell appeared and moved in his usual discreet fashion toward Wolsey. He slipped the note into the Cardinal's hand. The two exchanged a glance. Henry and Boleyn, meanwhile, moved in the center of the courtiers' circle: the King aware of the adulation all around him, and Boleyn equally aware of the courtiers' envy of the good fortune that greeted this new evidence of royal favor toward his house.

"Good, good," Henry was saying. "And when may I smell this pretty posy of yours?"

Boleyn hesitated for only an instant. "If you mean Anne, Sire, she is still at her mirror: a new dress, nervous fingers. If you could give her half an hour?"

Henry smiled at him expansively. "We've this whole day, Thomas."

"I've a new pack of hounds you may care to view. And there's a clump of red deer in the lower meadow—"

"We'll see the one and hunt the other!"

Wolsey cut in. "Good hunting, Your Grace."

The King turned to him. "You won't be with us?"

"Alas, Sire, no. It appears there are two poor souls who seek religious comfort," Wolsey replied in his gentlest prelate's tones. "I must go where I am called."

"Indeed, my lord Cardinal," the King remarked knowingly. "Indeed. God's work must come first." He gave Wolsey's elbow a little jostle. "And who knows," he added archly in a low voice, "there may be a little worldly profit attached."

"Sire!" Wolsey protested, chuckling.

The King, however, was on his way, striding out through the arch that led to the stables. Boleyn hurried beside him and the courtiers followed like a wave. Wolsey bowed in Henry's wake. Then he turned to Cromwell.

"Find them," he ordered. "Bring them to me." His face was impassive.

Cromwell's face was equally impassive as he hurried out on his errand. Wolsey looked after him, his red-gloved fingers tearing the note to shreds, which fell like snowflakes, like feathers, like wisps of cloud around his satin-shod feet.

25

King Henry, however, was unaware of all these ma-
neuvers behind him. He blithely progressed past the
stables and on to the kennels of Hever, with the master
of Hever in proud attendance. The courtiers followed,
talking among themselves and keeping a discreet distance.

The kennels were really of little interest to the King
that day. He was intent on the business at hand. "Now,
Thomas," he said, "a private word before I meet
Anne."

"Yes, Your Grace?"

For once, in spite of his customary bluffness, Henry
found himself unable to come to the point. "There's always a temptation for a man in my position," he
began, "to think of the nation as his own trough—and
get all four feet in and eat from one end to the
other—"

Boleyn broke in quickly. "Not Your Grace!" he
cried. His voice carried enough warmth and conviction
almost to convince himself, as he spoke, that his words
were not arrant hypocrisy.

"Why not?" Henry rejoindered. "Who can say *no* to
me except God? And He does, Thomas. That's the
point." He frowned. "I kneel, I pray, He answers. But
can that be seen to be so, Thomas?"

Boleyn's words fell like folds of silk. "Why else
would His Holiness the Pope have named you Defender of the Faith, Your Grace?"

Henry considered. "True. I am a religious man. I
wish to do right in the eyes of God and the church.
And myself. And my people. . . . And you, Thomas."
He grasped Boleyn's velvet tunic. "Do you follow?"

Boleyn's lips twitched into a smile to assure his sovereign that he intended a joke. "That's a swathe of folk
to satisfy—if you include God!"

"It includes your daughters, Thomas," he said heavily. "Tell me: are they friends?"

"Yes," Boleyn answered with a puzzled look in his
eyes.

The King's voice pressed closer to the point. "Do
they exchange confidences, do you think? Secrets, I

mean. Do they talk together at night, Anne and Mary?" His eyes narrowed. "About me, perhaps?"

Boleyn felt cornered. The game was getting tricky. "Who knows, Your Grace? The one you have had. The other you desire. I think you go a little rapidly with her. You'll need to be gentle with Annie."

Henry brushed his words aside. "Will Anne have me?" he demanded. "For myself, mind. She'll have me, in the end?"

"She's no fool, Sire," Boleyn said solemnly.

There was a long pause. The sky arched above them, Kent lay green all around them, and a day's hunting lay before them.

"What I do," Henry said at last, "is God's will. I tell you this first, Boleyn. God answers prayer. That's known. And every morning I go down on my knees and pray that what I do may be God's will. I pray Him to direct me, that whatever thought comes to my mind, whatever emotion floods my heart, shall be God's will, —and I, only His instrument. Wherever I turn, whatever I do, whether to reach for food or interpret the holy word, or judge men innocent or guilty: every morning I pray Him on my knees that nothing shall rise in my brain or heart but He has wished it first. And since He answers prayer, and since He's given me such heavy power to act, He must answer this." Henry paused and pressed his heavy finger against Boleyn's chest. "And He does answer, Thomas. I find such peace in this, that not one morning my whole life long shall I fail these devotions."

"That is a noble thought, Your Grace," Boleyn said, thinking rapidly. "But you realize that it might be used as an excuse for—"

"For what?" Henry cut in sharply.

"For doing as you please, for eating the trough dry."

"I'm quite serious, Boleyn," Henry said, a trifle peeved. "I want no trifling."

"It was not my intention to trifle," Boleyn hastily replied.

"But you do," the King persisted. "I tell you I pray and God answers!"

"Yes, Sire."

"I am younger than you, I am younger than Wolsey. I am younger than many of my dukes and earls and peers. But I am the King of England. When I pray, God answers."

"Yes, Sire," Boleyn said nervously.

"Let no man dare question it!"

Henry turned and made for the waiting circle of his companions.

Boleyn smiled a wry, private smile.

The King suddenly swung around.

"Nor woman either!" he called.

The circle of bright plumed hats surrounded him. Flattery and courtly words swept him forward, as on the crest of a wave. His hearty laughter filled the morning.

Six

In her pink morning dress, Anne raced through the gardens outside the castle. Above her arched the sky, beneath her feet lay the pebbled paths of her father's house, and before her Harry Percy suddenly burst out from behind a topiary hedge.

Laughing, they fell to the grass. Laughing, they kissed and broke and kissed again, panting and staring happily into each other's young morning faces.

Anne pressed her hands against Percy's chest and pushed him away from her. "I'm angry with myself about one thing," she told him.

"Yes, my dear. What?"

She regarded his handsome, raw, rough-hewn features. "I spent two years at the court of Queen Claude. I met there the flower of the French aristocracy. Such manners, such graces, such horsemanship and dancing! They spoke Greek, they spoke Latin, they spoke Italian—and they spoke their own tongue with a wit and fencer's point that gave me a new glimpse of what a language might be!"

He laughed. "What disappointed you, lass?"

"There were truly gallant men among them: captivating men, men with an ease of carriage and a way with women that—" She broke off. "And I fell in love with none of them. I came home and promptly fell in love with a—a thistle."

"Northern clodhopper, the King said," Harry reminded her.

She gazed dotingly at him. "A countryman from the North, with no graces at all. He can't dance. He can't sing. He can hardly speak English," Anne went on, touching his mouth tenderly with her long fingers.

"He can put his arms around you," he told her.

"Not as well as I've known it done," she replied, considering. "But for some God-knows-what reason, they are the arms I want. You do everything badly, everything awkwardly," she told him in a burst of fierceness, "and I love it the way you do it."

He laughed, but softly this time. "I'm glad I wasn't educated in France," he said.

"Why?" demanded Anne.

"You wouldn't have loved me," he said.

"I wonder," she said slowly, reflecting. "It may be true."

"Silks are for holiday," he went on gruffly. "Honest homespun wears through the years."

She pressed her hand against his lips. "One thing, though," she told him. He looked questioningly at her, and she went on. "If we love enough to marry, we must love enough to keep nothing back. I shall keep nothing from you."

"Nor I from you," he promised.

"But you have."

He frowned, puzzled.

"Are we to lie together?" he asked. "Before?"

"If you like," she said. "But that's not it."

"My bonny," he breathed, "what more can there be than that?"

"Kiss me hard!" she commanded.

He pressed his lips roughly against hers.

"I wish I had you in my house," he breathed.

"That's part of it, too," she told him, "to be Lady Anne, and live with you in your house, and sleep with you at night. And in the morning they'll bring in breakfast to the Earl, to Percy, the Earl of Northumberland, and his wife."

"Will you like that?" he asked anxiously.

"Yes," she said. "It's far from the court. It's buried in the Northern hills. But it's power, and I love you and I will like it." She looked again into his face. "Tell me," she said abruptly. "Are you a virgin?"

"I?" he asked, astonished.

"Yes, Harry of Northumberland, you!"

"I'm a man," he said roughly.

"I know. But are you a virgin? When we bed together, shall I be your first?" she insisted.

"I—I—" he stammered.

"Say it out," she told him. "For me, I'll say it all frankly, as they do in France. In England we make muddy mysteries of such things, as if they were crimes. But they've happened to all of us." She flicked her hand in a gesture of impatience. "We don't come out of a rainbow at seventeen and there's no use pretending we do." Her face was as tender and as open as the flowers in the Kentish countryside as she turned it toward him. "You may ask me whatever you like."

A long pause filled the spring air between them.

"Are you a virgin?" Percy asked at last.

"No," Anne answered.

They looked away from each other.

"In France? Was this something that happened there?" he asked in a harsh, remote voice.

"Yes," she answered slowly. "But long before France, too. When I was little I was playing with a boy in the woods not far from here. We quarreled about something, and he threw me down and—" She sprang

30

suddenly to her feet. "God help me," she cried. "I'm blushing! All over. I thought I'd finished with that." Her hands clenched into fists. "And I've told all this before!"

"Without blushing?" he asked, a little bitterly.

She tossed her head in defiance. "Yes!" she said. "But there's something in the torpid air of this island that makes people want to hide things."

"There might be another reason," he told her slowly.

She turned. "What?"

"Look at me," Percy commanded.

She obeyed.

He was not smiling when he spoke again. "Were you ever in love before?" he asked.

"I think—" she began. Then, "No," she cried. "No."

He said gravely in his slow Northern voice, "I'm no spring of wisdom in these matters, Anne, but it may be you're not a woman until you're in love. It may be you've nothing to hide till then."

"It may be," she echoed. "It's strange, Harry. I stand here still trying to say it to you, and it's a perfectly natural thing, and still my tongue won't say it."

"Never mind," he said. "I don't want to hear it. I don't like this game you learned in Paris."

She twisted around. "Were you an angel, then, up there in the North?" she asked mockingly.

"No. I was not."

"Tell me about the girls. How many, and when?" she went on.

"One thing you'd best learn now, my sweet," he told her stubbornly. "I'll be the man of the house when we have a house, and if any game's to be played, I'll lead in that game and not follow. And the game I like now is to put my arms about you and say nothing."

"You know," Anne said, "I think I like that better too." She laughed with joy and relief and moved back into his arms. "Come, then," she said happily.

At that moment a shadow moved toward them: a shadow cast by a slender clerkly figure in sober attorney's garb.

Anne put up a hand to hold Percy's lips back from hers.

"There is someone here," she whispered.

When they looked up, Thomas Cromwell stood there, thin-lipped, waiting to lead them back to the castle, to Wolsey, who wished to have a word with them.

Seven

Hand in hand they stood before the Cardinal in the library. The morning sun streamed through the tiny bull's-eye panes in the window. Outside, in the full sunshine, the King and his hunting party were in full cry after the red deer of Hever.

"I am glad I find you together," Wolsey said, "for I have to speak to you both." He turned to Percy. "My lord, your father and the King have given some thoughts to where you shall marry, and an alliance through the Talbots, through one of the daughters of the Earl of Shrewsbury, is thought best."

Percy stood for a moment, thunderstruck. Then he burst out, "An—alliance with—! Not by me, my lord Cardinal!" he cried.

It was as though Wolsey had not heard him. He turned his steel-colored eyes toward Anne. "Anne, my dear," he said, in a gentler tone, "your father has a claim on the Ormond estates in Ireland. He and the King have agreed that you will marry the Earl of Ormond to reinforce that claim." He raised his gloved hand to still the quick protest that rose to her lips. "Your father will deal with you," he went on. "As for Lord Percy, remember, if you will, that I brought you to court. You are still a member of my household. A half-grown steer and a leggy girl will not be allowed to overturn the policies of England, fixed in council."

"But, my lord," Harry Percy shouted, "I am of full age and I have pledged myself to this girl before many witnesses—among them her own father! It's a good match for both of us, and nothing has been said against it till this moment!" He caught the warning expression on the Cardinal's ruddy face, but he only lowered his voice and went on passionately. "More than that, we've pledged ourselves to each other, and our hearts go with that pledge!"

Wolsey gave him a chilly smile. "No doubt," he said. "And this is the reward I get for my kindness to you." He turned his face away.

Anne stepped forward. "My lord Cardinal," she said softly, "that we two are in love, and have been these two months, every servant in the house knows, for we've made no secret of it before them or anyone. That we are in love, that we mean to marry, has been no secret from the whole world all that time. Why have you come here now to tell us suddenly that we're to match elsewhere? There must be some reason behind it. Tell us what it is."

"I have told you," Wolsey answered.

Anne flared, "Then you talk nonsense, and I won't listen!"

"Nor I!" Percy shouted behind her.

Inside his red robes the Cardinal seemed to gather himself together and grow taller. "I stand here as the King's minister," he pronounced sternly, "and you're aware of that. I knew a great lord to die for less than you have just said. His name was Buckingham."

Percy's voice was humbler now as he said, "You know I have no wish to anger the King. But tell us what this means and why you say it to us."

"Do you think the King and I come lightly to such decisions as this?" Wolsey thundered. "Do you think we have not weighed every reason for and against before we issue a command? One thing I can tell you: you will obey or your estates are forfeit! If you continue disloyal, it is doubtful how long you will live! Go now, for I wish to speak to Anne alone."

Percy turned to the girl. "Anne—" he said, beseechingly.

"Yes," she said quietly. "You must go."

"Kiss me then," he told her.

Wolsey stepped forward. "Do not touch her!" he commanded.

Percy threw back his brown shoulders. "All this talk of sudden death makes it easy for you, my lord," he said in a firm voice. "But I shall kiss her if I like."

He leaned forward and pressed his lips against Anne's.

"Take care of yourself, Harry," she whispered. "I shall see you."

He turned and went out of the room, into the darkness of the corridors.

Now Anne stood looking at Wolsey, silent and defiant.

Wolsey permitted himself a wintry smile. "Look your knives through me, mistress," he told her. "At my age, it will do me no hurt, and at yours, though you hurt easily, you will cure quickly." Abruptly, he changed his tone. "Are you serious about this thornapple from the North?"

"My lord," she replied simply, "he's mine, and I am his."

"But if there were another and worthier, well, you could change?" he asked, his eyes narrowing craftily.

"No," she said.

"But I think when you see him you will," he said.

Anne released a short laugh. "The Earl of Ormond? Hardly!" she replied in scorn.

"That was only a name plucked out of the air," Wolsey went on, more gently. "I had another in mind."

"I want no other," she burst out. "And if you do him harm—I am only a girl, but you will know you have an enemy."

He folded his hands patiently. "Look down at your

necklace, Anne," he said. "Do you see a writing on it?"

She frowned. "There is no writing on it."

He shook his head. "There is, though, and I can see it, though it may not be visible to you as yet. It says: '*Noli me tangere,* for Caesar's I am.'"

"Caesar's?" she echoed scornfully.

The Cardinal remained immobile. "When Harry of England turns his eyes on a girl, she can hardly look away."

Anne gasped. There was a long pause between them. "Forgive me if I seem slow to understand what you say," she said at last. "Do you mean that King Henry has looked at me?"

Wolsey nodded slowly.

"And sent you to me?"

"It is sometimes my pleasure to anticipate his desires," Wolsey said, lowering his eyes.

"Even in carnal matters, my lord Cardinal?"

He did not reply.

"We have had the King in the bosom of this family for some years," she went on. "My sister Mary is with child with him, and of no further use to him at the moment." Her eyes flashed. "I shall not go the way of my sister. You would be wise," she told him, "to anticipate my answer and spare His Grace any annoyance." The veins in her temple throbbed under the thin white skin. "I will not be a mistress to the King, even with the blessing of a prince of the church!"

Wolsey regarded the angry girl who stood before him, measuring her youth, her beauty, her fury. The room was charged with their silence. When he spoke finally it was only to say, "You would be wise to consult your parents before the King returns."

She turned on her heel and left the room.

The Cardinal looked after her, thoughtfully, speculatively.

The door closed behind her.

Eight

Through the sun-dappled woods of Hever the hunting party made its way. It had been a good morning's chase. The red deer that had provided the King such good sport now were carried, dead, on poles, their heads dangling, their lusterless eyes fixed on the heels of the servants who bore them. Norfolk came first; then Mark Smeaton at Brereton's side. They were all on foot now: the King with his bow and quiver, the soldiers, the tired hounds. The courtiers strode along at a good pace, for the King was cheerful.

The towers of Hever hung in the air in the near distance.

"Good sport in Hever's woods!" Henry cried in a roar of satisfaction.

"And in Boleyn's bowers, he hopes," Norris remarked to Weston, who walked beside him.

"I hear you, Norris," Henry called over his shoulder. He stopped and waited for Norris and Weston to come up to him. "Well, you buzz the girls, you two," he said, clapping his broad hands on their shoulders. "Tell me, man to man, kingship aside. You've thrust your hands in amongst a flutter of larks often enough and pulled out the one you wanted. What's the best way to win a maiden?"

Weston grinned. "A virgin, Your Grace?"

"I couldn't swear to it, medically," the King countered with good humor. "But a young one," he added. "And wild."

Weston's grin widened.

"My King," he said, "my skills are not for the grade of female you seek. I'm more successful with waiting-women and ladies' maids."

The King threw back his head and laughed. "Don't be modest, lad," he roared. "I've followed your spoor so close there was scarce time to close the window you left by, or change perfumes to put me off the scent. Speak on. Your lure, your most seductive!"

"You'll not be offended?" Weston asked.

"I'll be offended if you hold back," the King assured him.

"Why, then, if you truly want her," Weston said jovially, "make her believe you're potent only with her. Pretend that you've tried with numbers of others, gone to bed and kissed hotly and hung embarrassed and unable. But with her you rouse up. You're a man again." The others burst into raucous laughter. "They can't resist that," Weston went on. "They open like—"

"Never mind the simile," Henry shouted, cutting into Weston's speech. "There's nothing like it. Ha! What a gambit!" The flesh puckered around his eyes as he too burst into laughter.

Norris spoke. "Dare I ask, has Your Grace ever been refused by a maid?"

"Refused? I, Harry? Never!" Henry rejoindered. "When I've wanted them I've had them. And once I've had a wench, I'm cured. That's general, isn't it?"

Through their laughter, Norfolk's voice came, calling from the head of the procession.

"Your Grace," he cried, cupping his hands to his mouth, "can you youngsters leave talking of virgins long enough to look at the venison?"

Henry nudged his companions. "Yes," he called. "Come. Next to a haunch of a virgin, there's nothing like a haunch of venison!"

The laughter redoubled as the gallant party strode off toward Hever.

Nine

The Boleyns were gathered in the great hall at Hever. They were all there, except for Mary who, forlorn and disconsolate, lay in her bedroom watching her belly grow bigger with the King's child.

Anne stood at bay. She faced her parents. A terrible anger twisted her face and her voice was deliberately loud as she spoke to them. "Do you also offer me up to this royal bull?" she demanded. "You, my father, and you, my mother?"

Boleyn shuddered. He was aware of Thomas Cromwell standing in the background, in the shadow of the staircase. "For God's sake," he said, "lower your voice."

She refused to lower it. "Do you know what it is to be in love, either of you?" she cried in a fury. "I love Harry Percy, and I will marry him!"

George Boleyn moved to his sister's side. He looked at her fondly. He spoke softly and urgently to her. "Anne, you'll have us all dead or disgraced. Lower your voice. Be devious. The royal bull can't *force* you."

She turned her head toward him. Her look was wild. "Brother," she cried, "I must fight, I must."

Lady Elizabeth spoke, her hands fluttering in dismay. She had spent her life witnessing the courtier's game, the victim and partner of Boleyn's ambition. "Do you know what it means when a king asks for you?"

"If I don't," Anne flashed back, "I can ask my pregnant and foolish sister."

"If you turn him away," Lady Elizabeth said in a worn, tired voice, "we can say farewell to all we've worked for and all we have."

George spoke again. "Anne," he told her, "if our parents had not taken an advantage when it came their way, what would have become of us?"

It was Boleyn's turn now. "If we lose the King's favor," he said ominously, "we lose everything."

"Then say good-bye to it all," the girl cried. "House, rank, and revenues, for I will not take the King to my bed."

"He is a great king," her father put in anxiously. "Handsome, brave, and generous. Surely it's not hard to think well of him?"

"I'm trying to think well of him," Anne shot back angrily, "but he's been married for seventeen years. If all his children—legitimate and illegitimate—had lived, there would be at least a dozen. He can only be *fairly* faithful to a mistress. I think my sister Mary kept him the longest. That lasted four years. Now that's over. And what becomes of Mary? No, I won't ask that. It's true that his father, who was unscrupulous and a miser, left him a mountain of money. It's true therefore that he has great power, but as for his being a great king, I say he is neither wise nor just nor merciful. He's much praised for his poetry and music at the court, where, if you don't praise him, you're likely to be unlucky. You say he speaks and dances better than any about him. Wouldn't it be a silly courtier who outdanced the proud Henry? And when it comes to warfare, his wife Katherine is a better soldier: she won the battle of Flodden Field while he was abroad subjugating two minor French towns with an army sufficient to conquer all Europe! He—"

Thomas Cromwell's voice, sharp and warning, broke into Anne's tirade.

"Your Grace!"

Henry stood in the doorway to the hall.

Terror froze the faces of Boleyn and Lady Elizabeth. George grasped Anne's hand to give her support.

39

There was no knowing how long Henry had been standing there.

The King looked from one to another, smiling. His eyes rested last on Anne. He was panting slightly. Then, suddenly, Henry broke the ominous silence. He moved toward Lady Elizabeth, his laugh ringing out. "I was so anxious to see *you*, Madam, that I ran ahead!" He gave her a hearty buss. "Been faithful to me? Or have you been lying around with this husband of yours?" Their laughter filled the room—his hearty, hers nervous—as he directed a lusty slap at her skirts. Even Boleyn joined in their laughter, his sycophantic eyes watching the King warily.

"Remarkable women you breed, you Howards!" the King cried out.

And now the rest of the party came through the door in a burst of talk and laughter. The Duke of Norfolk was among those in the forefront. "Norfolk," the King called. "Greet your sister!"

Norfolk advanced and kissed Lady Elizabeth.

"You see, Madam," the King said, "I brought your brother to make sure I'm welcome." He turned to George then. "You should have hunted with us, not stayed at home with the women," he told him.

As he spoke, he stretched out his hand for young Boleyn to kiss. But all the time, while he spoke and laughed and jested, his eyes had been on Anne. And now they faced each other. The elder Boleyns stood watching tensely. Cromwell looked on with cool interest, and the courtiers stood by expectantly. There was a brief pause while Henry and Anne confronted each other, eye to eye. Then Anne began to sink into a curtsy.

Henry reached his hand out to take hers, stopping her.

"Nan," he said, "will you give me a kiss?"

There was another pause while necks craned, and even the whispering in the outermost ranks was stilled.

"Yes, Your Grace," the girl replied.

He stretched out his arms to embrace her, a jovial smile on his bearded face. He had given his orders, the girl was here before him, and by tonight they would be

bedded together. There were no doubts as to the outcome of this hunting party to Hever!

Anne moved gracefully to one side, bowed over one
of his outstretched hands, and kissed it.

Henry cocked his head. "It was not such a kiss I
meant, my dear." He was taken aback, but quick to
guard his pride. "And now the lips, sweet Nan," he
said.

Anne lowered her eyes. "I have been drinking foul
medicines for a cold, Sire. You would never forgive
my breath."

This was an opposition that left Henry undaunted.
He knew well enough how to play the game. "Have
you tried hippocras, a strong glassful every hour,
steaming hot?"

"I have not, Sire."

He moved forward a step. "Your health is very dear
to me," he murmured. "You must keep well. We live
all too brief a time, Nan. What little we have should
not be wasted." Suddenly he stooped and kissed her
lips. "There is neither fever not medicine on your lips,
sweetheart, but such a honey scent—!"

Anne stood rigid, holding herself with the impecca-
ble politeness and formality of a loyal subject. "The
overwhelming surprise of Your Grace's visit," she replied, with a bow, "must have cured me."

Henry stood back for a moment, taking in the reaction of all those present in the hall. There was a hush
all around them, as though the others were holding
their breath to see what the King's next move would
be.

He smiled. The white plume nodded in his hat.

"Shall I send away this chaperonage that rings us
round?" he demanded.

"No," she cried quickly, "by your leave!"

"I will, though, by your leave; no, without your
leave!" He swung around on the assembled company.
"Mothers, fathers, sons, lawyer"—this last with a curt
nod to Cromwell—"and companions, out! Depart!" He
went striding around the hall, driving them all toward
the doors. The departure was so precipitous as to be
almost unseemly. And when all the others had finally

41

pushed their way out of the King's presence, he was left standing the whole hall's width from Anne.

The doors slammed to.

Henry looked across the hall to where Anne waited, pale and immobile. Only her clenched hands betrayed her distressed state.

When he spoke now, the bluster was gone from his voice. "You would never credit how fast my heart beats," he said, "nor how hard it is to draw breath. Nan, I come to you as frightened as a 'prentice who takes his first nosegay to a wench."

"I see the King," she answered.

"Trust me," he pleaded. "A king is not fortunate in these matters. Whether you like me or not, whether any woman likes me or not, I shall never know. I shall never be sure I have the truth because I am the King, and love is paid to me like taxes. Do me this favor, Nan. Look on me not as a monarch who commands and may demand, but as the doubting, hoping, tremulous man I am—wishing to be loved for myself."

He had come close to her and was about to put an arm about her. She made no effort to move away or to resist him.

"If you were a common man," she said, "doubtful of yourself and tremulous, would you have sent me an old church pander to give me my orders?"

He took his arm away as if it had been stung.

"Pander!"

"Lord Cardinal Wolsey speaks for you, I believe."

"Did he speak clumsily?"

"No, very deftly. He made it plain that what the King wanted he would have."

"Then he was clumsy. I swear to you, Anne. It is quite the reverse. What *you* want is what you shall have."

His arm curved around her once again.

"If I have you first," she reminded him.

"Not against your will!"

"Not?" The word was edged with mockery.

"Never!" he told her.

She stepped away, moving clear of his arm.

"I'll earn your love and then your bed," the King

cried. "Are there things you want? Name them. Prove me!"

"There is one thing I want," she replied evenly. "I want something that has gone from here."

"You shall have it!" he swore. "Now walk with me. Talk with me, Nan. I love your company and your sweet voice and bold spirit." He took her arm. "Tell me, dare I ask it, is there anything about me you love?"

"No."

"By God!" he cried.

Her face remained still and grave. "You asked not to be treated like the King. I would have lied to the King."

He stared at her. "No woman has ever said that to me," he exclaimed. "By God!"

"My sweet voice will not lie to you."

He stroked his beard. A small smile curved on his lips. "But in time, Nan," he told her, "you'll grow to love me."

"Anything is possible," she countered coolly.

His eyes narrowed. His smile grew broader. He placed his arm once more about her waist and this time he left it there.

"With us, my sweet Nan, everything is possible!" he said on an exulting note.

Ten

Hidden in the shadow in the minstrel gallery, Wolsey and Cromwell watched and listened.

They saw Anne with the King's arm around her. They heard Henry's laughter ring out as the pair walked the length of the hall and out of sight.

Against the livid hue of the Cardinal's face, his teeth showed in a pleased smile. "Well, that's settled," he said. "I can return to London."

"And I, my Lord?" Cromwell asked.

"You will remain here."

"Here, my Lord?"

"To keep me informed."

Cromwell nodded.

Wolsey moved his bulk, preparing to leave.

"Do you think the King truly loves her?" Cromwell said. He spoke almost idly, although his brain was racing.

"My dear Cromwell," the Cardinal replied with a short enigmatic laugh, "you heard the King himself. Everything is possible."

His robes rustled as he departed. His laugh still echoed in Cromwell's ears as he remained behind in the shadows, thinking.

It was a long time since his first meeting with the Cardinal at Hampton Court, seeing that magnificent palace grouping itself around its creator with a perfect appropriateness. The largeness of the Cardinal's style and the ease with which he bore it had burned itself upon the young clerk's mind. This was a master; and in Cromwell's soul had been fired the desire to be his servant.

And Wolsey too had recognized that the man at his feet was malleable and eager to serve. Here was a plebeian—unlike the nobles who resented the greatness of a butcher's son. Cromwell was a useful man, capable, without the fantasy of a hereditary lord who emulated the King. He was a roundheaded, crop-eared man of the people with hard clear eyes. For the Cardinal he would be a man to depend on: a quick-witted, sure-footed agent, flexible and audacious.

From that day, Thomas Cromwell had been the apprentice of Wolsey's mind, whose honesty Wolsey might doubt but whose ability could never be questioned.

Now, in the musicians' gallery at Hever, sheltered by arras and shadow, Wolsey's man stood deep in thought.

Eleven

The rose-colored glory of Wolsey's palace at Hampton Court once again smote Cromwell's eyes as he approached it. The towers shone in the sun; the gardens were as amazing to him as they had been the first day he had caught sight of them—that momentous day when he had become the Cardinal's man. Now, even though the Italianate pile with its terra cottas and its splendor that equaled anything in the King's possession had become a familiar sight, it still awed him. It was the symbol of a greatness and a power and a way of life that never failed to take his breath, even though he knew all that lay behind it.

Today, however, there was no time to cast his crafty glance anywhere except on the path and the corridors that would lead him to the Cardinal. For he had come up from Hever Castle bringing the news that his master awaited.

As he stood in the doorway of the Cardinal's room, he could see Wolsey sitting at his desk, a scarlet cap covering his short grizzled hair, his dropsical body heavy in his chair, his florid face bent over a pile of state papers. At another desk sat Sir Thomas More, equally intent. Around them buzzed a hive of busy secretaries. Messengers moved among them, bringing papers, taking others away. As Cromwell stood there, one messenger brushed past him, running out of the room. Wolsey, without raising his head, called after him, "And tell my lord of Suffolk that we shall entertain no more such petitions."

Cromwell walked over to the Cardinal's desk.

Wolsey turned to a secretary and handed him a paper. "Show that to Sir Thomas More," he ordered. "That's in his province." Then he looked up and said pleasantly to Cromwell, "Thomas, you smell of horse-sweat!"

Cromwell acknowledged the greeting with a dry, businesslike nod. "His Grace has sent me to inform you, my lord," he said, "that the entertainment at Hever suits him well. And he intends to remain."

"Excellent!" Wolsey said. A secretary handed him a sheet of paper. His eyes read the writing in a second. "No," he told the secretary, handing the paper back, "tell Lovell his request is denied."

Cromwell went on: "That witch has been leading him a dance for two weeks now."

"She will go the way of all the rest," the Cardinal observed shortly. He held out another paper to the waiting secretary. "Granted," he said.

Cromwell's brows knitted almost imperceptibly. "The King should be here," he said, "attending to matters of state, not pursuing a reluctant girl. If he wants her, he should take her. He is the King."

More had risen and joined them.

"Ha!" the Cardinal exclaimed. "What is Sir Thomas More's opinion about that?"

More's candid eyes, set deep in his bony ascetic face, rested for a moment on Wolsey's. Then he turned to Cromwell. "Master Cromwell," he said gently, "when you counsel the King, tell him what he ought to do, but never what he is able to do. If he knew his real strength it would be hard for any man to rule him."

"He ought to leave Hever," Cromwell said stubbornly.

"Let sleeping kings lie, Thomas," Wolsey told him, "and *we'll* see to the government of the country."

He turned then and spoke to More of other matters, leaving Cromwell to turn over in his restless, ever-calculating mind the words the Cardinal had said so lightly, smiling.

Twelve

The days continued fair at Hever. The King stayed on: an exacting but welcome guest; a persistent and pressing suitor.

Anne and the King rode out of the castle that morning, their horses' hooves clattering over the drawbridge. Anne rode well, sitting lightly on her mount. The King sat squarely on his steed, spurring it to a gallop as he pursued her.

Through the thick woods of Hever they rode, and down beside the water. At a small stone bridge their horses stopped. The King dismounted first and lifted Anne down from her mare. His heavy hands enclosed her waist. She remained still, indifferent.

"It's a cruel thing," Henry burst out, "to be near a woman day by day, to touch her when you want to, to have her company when you ask it, but to have no response; to burn with love as I do for you and be denied pleasure in your cool company. It's a cruel thing, Anne, to be denied love!"

"The same cruel thing has happened to me," she answered quickly. "I have fallen in love."

His eyes blazed. "Anne!"

"But not with you."

He took his hands from her waist and stepped back.

"By God!" he shouted. "I got it full in the face that time! Who is it! Northumberland?"

"You know well enough. You had Wolsey send him away," she said.

"Love!" he cried scornfully. "With that young blundering wattle and daub—"

"I mean to marry him," she said, flushing.

"Never."

"But not as my sister is married," Anne went on resolutely. "He won't be a complaisant husband. And I would not be an accessible wife."

"All wives are accessible," Henry retorted hotly. "Any husband can be placated—even a Percy of Northumberland!"

"Then you have nothing to fear, Your Grace! Let me marry him."

"No! I don't want you that way. I want all of you to myself. Nan, give him up, I tell you, and this kingdom shall turn round you, bishops and peers—and whatever you've wanted, for anyone, a knighthood, an estate, a great income rolling in forever, titles and places, you shall dispose of them exactly as you please!"

Her mouth curled angrily. "And be thrown out in the end like a dirty rag?" she countered. "I haven't seen my sister Mary disposing of great revenues."

"Mary asked for nothing. Look, Anne. I stand here desperate. I can't bargain with you. Ask for what you want."

She flung her head back. Her neck was slim and white and slender. "To be free!" she cried. "To be free to marry where I love!"

Henry paused. He looked at her longingly, then at the ground. The jewels in his hat glittered in the sunshine.

"No!" he said at last.

Her anger flared higher. "I've seen you too close and known you too long," she bit out. "I've heard what your courtiers say and then I've seen what you are. You're spoiled and vengeful and bloody. The poetry they praise is sour, and the music you write is worse. You dance like a hobbledehoy. You make love as you eat—with a good deal of noise and no subtlety—"

"Take care!" he warned.

"It was my doubtful pleasure once to sleep in Mary's room," she went on, unheeding, "or to lie

48

awake when you thought me asleep and observe the royal porpoise at play."

He breathed heavily. "This is not safe!" he cried out in exasperation.

"Yes," she went on recklessly, "I've been told it's not safe for any of us to say 'no' to our Squire Harry, that put-on, kindly, hail-fellow-well-met of yours. My father's house will be pulled down, and Northumberland's too, they tell me. Well, pull them down. You are what I said."

There was a long pause. Henry's face was mottled as he struggled to control the terrible anger that had mounted in him.

"I had no wish to come here," he said in a cold, remote voice. "I came because I must, and couldn't help myself. Well, I'm out of it. Let it end here this morning." He gave her a bitter smile. "I thank you for your anger, and for raising anger in me. There's no better way to make an end." He turned and mounted his horse.

For the first time Anne felt a contraction of fear in her heart. Her pulse was pounding.

"You will not—touch—Northumberland?" she cried.

"I'll try not," he answered in a voice like a blade of ice. "Vengeful and bloody as I am, I'll try not."

He wrenched his horse's head around, dug in his spurs, and galloped off, the white plume in his velvet hat waving against the green of the Kentish fields.

Thirteen

Lady Elizabeth poked the fire in the library. However bright the sun might be outside, the rooms of Hever were always a little chilly. She was worried. Would the luck of the Howards hold, now with Mary sulking and heavy with the King's child, no longer the toy he had played with; and with Anne, whom the King wanted as he had never wanted Mary, holding him off in a bold game that could come to no good?

A horse's hooves rattled on the drawbridge outside Rising wearily, she went to the window. A mud-spattered horseman galloped over the bridge and disappeared into the courtyard. She shook her head: what was there to expect in days like these but ill news and tidings to turn the hair grayer?

She hurried out to the corridor and down the stairs.

In the courtyard, meanwhile, a servant had stopped the rider's mount, asking, "Where are you from?"

"Northumberland," came the answer. "I've a message for Lady Anne."

The exhausted rider flung himself from the horse. More servants in Hever's livery came running out to see to the horse, which was blown and sweating heavily.

"You'd best get some rest," the first servant told the messenger. "Give me the letter."

He took it from his leather pouch. "Give it only to the Lady Anne," he instructed.

The servant nodded and hurried toward the house with it.

Elizabeth Boleyn stood in the doorway. He stopped as he saw her there. Her hand was held out to receive the letter.

For a moment the man hesitated. Then he held it out.

Lady Elizabeth took it from him without a word and went back into the castle.

It was night before Lady Elizabeth went up to Anne's room. She went alone.

Anne was there, pacing. She had written to Northumberland in secret. "I've sent him away," she had written. "Take care of yourself. But for God's sake, come if you can—for I'm alone." And she had waited alone in her little room, where it had been her father's pleasure to keep her prisoner.

Lady Elizabeth went in without knocking. Anne was pale and haggard in the firelight. Silently, Elizabeth handed Anne the letter.

"You've brought word from Harry at last!"

Her mother said nothing.

She read it. And then, weeping, she threw herself onto her bed. "Harry Percy is to be married!" she cried. She picked up the letter again and read it with unbelieving eyes. "I'm a prisoner too," it said. "And I'm to be married to the Shrewsbury hag. She hates me and I hate her. One of us will murder the other. I'm afraid God's on her side and she'll kill me first. Anne, my bonny, forgive me."

Anne left off her weeping and said, hard-eyed, "The King did this!"

"Not the King," her mother put in. "Wolsey. See here, where he says 'I would have held out, but for your safety, dearest Anne—' "

"My safety?"

Elizabeth nodded gravely. "That would be Wolsey's threat: that you would suffer if Percy remained defiant."

Anne pressed her palms to her burning face. "Oh, God!" she cried. "I can't believe it. The pain is so great I want to die!"

Elizabeth stooped and held her daughter closely.

"The pain goes, my child," she said in a quiet, strangled voice. "Few of us marry where our hearts lie. When I was young and at the court I loved the King."

Anne raised her head. "You?"

Her mother nodded. "It all came to nothing. None of you children are his. I was never his mistress—but I would have been had he asked."

Anne beat her hands against the bedclothes. "I shall never see Harry again," she wailed. Her tears turned after a while to fury. "Sometime, somehow," she cried, "I shall repay His Grace Cardinal Wolsey. I shall!" And then, in a little while, her fury turned back to tears.

Elizabeth Boleyn said nothing. She only looked down with pitying eyes at her unhappy child and pressed Anne's head against her breast.

Fourteen

King Henry paced no room like a prisoner. He made free use of London, using his city like a private bawdy house in which he might forget the girl who had defied him. His only desire was to erase her haunting face and voice.

But wherever he went—into the low houses along the river; into the taverns where he watched the wrestlers maim each other to win the coppers that were thrown their way; or wenching with Norfolk, Norris, Brereton, and Weston—her face was there, her taunts rang in his ears.

Nothing pleased him—not girls, not wine, not feasting, not sport. Pleasure itself was stale in his mouth.

Why must he want this one girl who did not want him?

And he slept badly for thinking of her. Or he could not sleep at all and sat awake writing poems that did not please him either.

Then one day he knew that there was nothing to do but to return to Hever.

He had to see Anne Boleyn.

Fifteen

At Hever there were great preparations afoot.

The great hall was being readied for a banquet and dance. The tables and stools had already been set out. The servants marched in bearing the wine and the bread and the knives, the encrusted goblets, the household's best platters. On the walls were new hangings, chief among them being an enormous tapestry into which had been woven the royal coat of arms. In the midst of all the running and bustle stood Lady Elizabeth in a gown that was stiff with newness.

Boleyn, the Master of Hever, came racing down the great stairs, calling to his wife.

She met him at the foot of the stairs.

"Elizabeth," he said urgently, "for God's sake, go up to her. Make her hurry. The King is hungry, and when he's hungry he's evil-tempered. Leave this to me." They exchanged a glance.

Her skirt held up in her hands, Elizabeth started up the stairs, leaving Boleyn to fume at the servants.

Already the wall torches were being lit.

Elizabeth passed the book-room. Through the door she could hear Mark Smeaton singing. Then his voice broke off in mid-phrase as the King bellowed, "No! No! No! No!"

The door was slightly ajar, and she peered through the crack. There stood Henry, richly dressed, with a splendid chain of gold and jewels around his neck. The musicians had all gathered there and were concentrating on him. Smeaton held a song in his hand. And Henry, as anxious as a sixteen-year-old swain come a-wooing for the first time, was imparting his instructions.

"Gravely, Smeaton," he said. "With deep feeling. My God, it may lack greatness, but it sings what is in my heart. Like this, like this!" He signaled impatiently to the musicians and began to sing:

"Farewell, farewell my pleasure past,
Welcome my present pain,
Welcome the torment in my heart
To see my love again."

He turned and struck the sheet of music with his hand. "From the heart, Smeaton. We must touch the lady!"

Lady Elizabeth listened no more but sped on to Anne's room. There, Anne was being helped to dress by a maid, while her sister Mary, her belly distended and her face sallow, sat nearby.

"The sacrifice being decked out for the royal bull," Anne called out when she glimpsed her mother. "Is Wolsey with him?"

"No," Elizabeth told her. She nervously adjusted the fastenings on Anne's dress. Anne fidgeted. "Keep still," Lady Elizabeth said. "I can hardly believe that he has returned."

"He wants what he cannot have," Mary said sourly.

"And will continue to want," Anne retorted.

"Make yourself pretty, Anne," Mary said. Her voice

54

no longer held a bitter edge. "Whatever you want, you can have it now. He has never returned to a woman before."

"Lucky for all of us," their mother put in. "Not least for the child you're going to have. Henry is always generous with his children."

Mary ignored her mother. "Learn from me, Nan. Lock up your heart. Never surrender yourself completely." She shifted her weight painfully. "When he came to me first, he was still naïve. He was afraid of women who might be difficult. He wanted someone to whom he could say 'open!' and she'd open. That's what attracted him to me. He said 'open!' and there I was: his—his mule. It's his own word."

"You may yet be the mother of a king of England," her mother reminded her.

Mary shook her head. "Small chance of that," she said. "And small reward in it."

Anne said, holding her head very high, "I shall never surrender myself at all."

"If you ever go to him," Mary told her, "remember to keep a cold reserve of hate and anger and—"

"Thank you," Anne interrupted. "I shall not go to him."

"From the moment you are won and conquered and a worshiper, he'll give you back to yourself and walk away. He'll want no more of you."

"I shan't go to him, nor let him come to me. I'm not sure—"

"That's enough!" Lady Elizabeth cried angrily.

Anne said slowly, "I hated him from the beginning. I hate him now. I hate him only a little less than I hate Wolsey."

Boleyn burst into the room. His eyes were anxious but his manner was bright and cheerful. "Ready?" he asked.

"I am quite ready, Father," Anne replied.

"I think the King is waiting and anxious," Boleyn said.

Anne moved first, sweeping through the door. The Boleyns exchanged a signal, then moved out into the corridor behind her.

The door swung closed. Mary remained there alone with her swollen belly, not hating Anne, not even hating Henry, only miserable and bored and unable to believe that the King had changed toward her. Through the door she could hear the distant music. How short a time had passed, the girl thought, since the music and the singing had been for her!

The great hall blazed with light. The presence of the King and his entourage had altered it. It was now the court. Anne sat beside Henry at the feast. And finally, when the broken meats littered the tables, and much of the wine had been drunk, Smeaton stood with the musicians and sang Henry's song:

> "Farewell, farewell, my pleasure past,
>   Welcome my present pain,
> Welcome the torment in my heart
>   To see my love again.
>
> "Alone, alone, I longer for her,
>   All mistresses forsaking.
> Now must I tell my hopes and fear
>   Of love in her awaking."

The applause when Smeaton had ended was loud and protracted. Even the musicians joined in. All cast looks of admiration and congratulation at the King. Only Anne did not applaud.

Henry did not fail to notice this.

Boleyn spoke hastily to cover his daughter's lapse. "Bravo, Your Grace!"

Elizabeth joined in. "No other king in Europe can write as you do, Your Grace!"

"That cheers me, Elizabeth," the King said. He pressed his lips into a little pout. "Something was said at one time—I forget by whom—about my bad poetry and limping music."

"No!" Boleyn protested.

Henry brushed his protest aside. His gaze was still concentrated on Anne. "It rankled deep," he went on. "But then I saw that there was only one answer: to write great poetry and great music. Since I have a cause for anguish in my life, and songs come out of

56

anguish, I have heard these strains in the night when I woke out of sleep, and I have risen and written them down. Many songs came to me. This is only one. When I hear it, I know it sings what is in my heart—the pain and the loss and the parting that's like death. It carries the burden of a grief."

Anne raised her hand briefly to her mouth to conceal a yawn.

Henry's voice rose. "If some young man had written this song for you, Anne—what would you say of it?"

"I would ask him how his wife liked it, your Grace."

All those near enough to hear drew in their breaths. The gasp was audible. The astounded silence spread out to the courtiers who sat beyond the small group that surrounded Henry, out to the musicians. Not even a whisper could be heard as Henry rose to his feet.

His eyes were fixed on Anne. "You shall dance to my tune, mistress," he told her. Then he called out to the musicians, "The basse dance I composed—play!" He turned his countenance on the whole company. "Be merry!" he shouted. "Dance!"

He took Anne by the hand and led her to the floor. All the others were moving to take their places. The musicians struck up the melody and the dance began.

"Anne," he said, "why do you taunt me?" His eyes were pained.

Her brow remained unfurrowed. "Has Your Grace heard the latest gossip? Sir Harry Percy has married the Shrewsbury hag."

"Not my doing," he answered gruffly.

"I see." Anne considered. "Wolsey is the King of England, is he?"

Suddenly he pulled her by the hand, dragging her away from the dancers until they stood behind a large carved screen.

"That's enough!" he told her harshly. "I am the King. If you dare to treat me like a boring boy before my court I'll pull this castle down about your ears—"

"Do so!" she taunted.

They faced each other fiercely.

Henry said, "I have learned something that makes me very humble, Nan. Even a king cannot choose where he will love. I didn't want to come here. But here I am."

"Even if I loved you," she returned scornfully, "you offer me nothing. You're not free."

"Not free?"

"You are married to Katherine."

"Does that matter to a king? A king makes his own rules."

"Does he? A king or no king, if he's married, he's not free."

"If you loved me, you'd find me free."

She smiled contemptuously. "From your marriage?"

"Here is my marriage, Nan. My older brother Arthur was heir to the kingdom. To make an alliance with Spain he married Katherine of Aragon. Then Arthur died, and I was heir. To continue the alliance with Spain I was advised to marry Arthur's widow, six years my senior. And I did. At eighteen I married her. I never loved her. I never should have married my brother's widow. There's a curse on the marriage. We cannot have sons. Our sons are all born dead. There is no male heir to the English crown because of this accursed union. For twenty years I have had dead sons. The kingdom faces anarchy when I die and I face anarchy in my own life, because I have no male heir—yet because of the church and our friendship with Spain I remain Katherine's husband. What has this barren marriage to do with you and me?" He broke off, letting his blazing eyes rest on her unmoved face.

There was a pause before she spoke. Then she said simply, "You cannot touch my heart. You cannot bribe me with favors. The only love I will give you is the love of a loyal subject for her king."

The blaze in his eyes became a bonfire.

"Very well then," he said quietly. "As your king I command you to return with me to the court. I command you to be lady-in-waiting to my wife Katherine. You will be in my presence every day of your life. And then we shall see!"

She lowered her eyes. She made a low curtsy. It was her only reply.

Sixteen

Anne Boleyn went to Greenwich to be lady-in-waiting to Queen Katherine.

It did not take her long, accustomed as she was to the gay activity of the court of France, to find her duties monotonous, if not irksome. Katherine still dressed in the stiff, somber Spanish fashion. She had little taste for the hunting and dancing and lighthearted activities that Henry enjoyed with his courtiers. And she spent much of her day in devotions, kneeling in the chapel and praying for the boy-child that Henry wanted, while her ladies-in-waiting knelt patiently behind her, wearing on their faces expressions of devoutness while their thoughts wandered.

On this day of bright sunshine Anne felt particularly pent as, the last in the row of Katherine's ladies, she remained on her knees in the dark chapel. The candles flickered in front of her eyes. The air was close. Was it here that she was destined to spend the years of her youth, in the train of this austere Spanish matron to whom happiness and joy had always been, and would forever be, strangers?

Suddenly, the chapel door opened silently. In its frame stood Anne's brother, George, filling it with the breath of the cheerful lively world outside. Anne turned her head and George beckoned to her. Anne got to her feet and moved quietly away. When the Queen had crossed herself and rose, she caught a glimpse of the door closing softly behind the two Boleyns.

Katherine clasped her hands more tightly together and looked down, overwhelmed by a new wave of melancholy. She knew where Anne was bound and who had sent for her.

Hand in hand, Anne and George ran past the guards along the path that led to the palace gardens. Their voices were as clear and as uninhibited as children's.

"Was he shouting for me?" Anne demanded.

"Bellowing!"

She giggled. "How they all tremble when he bellows!"

"And you?" George asked.

Anne stopped in her tracks. She held out her hand with the fingers outspread.

"Does that tremble?" she demanded.

"No," he admitted. "But you so hated coming here. You spoke so wildly! I feared you might provoke his worst anger."

"That was six months ago," she reminded him. "I'm still young." Her voice soared. "I love dancing and new clothes and gifts—and power!"

Her brother gave her a startled glance.

Anne's eyes sparkled. "Power is as exciting as love, I discover. And who has more of it than the King?"

Her laughter rang out as they ran gaily off together.

In another part of the gardens, in the archery court, Henry took aim at a large standing target. He released the bowstring, and the arrow flew straight into the bull's-eye. He marked it with a glint of satisfaction. Then he reached for another arrow from the quiver which his archer held for him.

At his left elbow stood Wolsey. The King might disport himself at archery, but for Wolsey it was part of his own working day. Cromwell was there to hand him the documents that needed to be brought to the King's attention. Two secretaries stood in attendance, each with a portable desk slung from his neck, bearing quill, inkhorn, paper, and sanders. One of the secretaries wrote away busily. And not far away, shooting at other targets, Weston and Norris awaited the King's pleasure.

Wolsey held up a document that was waiting to be sent off. "The warship will be launched from the main yard at Portsmouth in the five days' time, Your Grace. Here is the warrant, but a name is needed for the vessel."

"The Anne Boleyn," the King replied without hesitation, as he fired the arrow at the target.

The warrant was passed to the second secretary, who proceeded to write in the name.

Wolsey resumed smoothly, "The ambassadors from Spain, from His Holiness the Pope, are seeking audience."

"Deal with them yourself," the King told him brusquely.

He had seen Anne and George approaching and strode forward to meet her.

"She almost reigns, she entirely rules," Cromwell said in a low voice to Wolsey. "And, I believe, gives nothing for it. She could prove powerful."

"Thomas," the Cardinal answered blandly, "this is a man's world. The seat of power does not lie between a woman's legs."

The King approached, holding Anne's arm, with George following several paces behind them. There was a young man's spring to Henry's gait, and the plume floated bravely in his velvet hat.

"Wolsey!" he cried. "Nan reminds me that her father's patent to be Earl of Wiltshire has not yet been drawn."

Wolsey bowed his head slightly. "It shall be done at once, Your Grace."

Anne looked at Wolsey for a moment. Then she began to laugh.

He smiled back, guardedly, at her.

Her peals of laughter only rang our louder.

"I must tell you, my lord," she said to him, "of a game we ladies-in-waiting play: a game of titles. Who has the most titles in the land?" She turned to Henry. "I said that it was, of course, the King. But another said, 'No, no. The great Cardinal Wolsey has more than the King, for he is Bishop of Tournai, of Lincoln, of Bath, of Wells, of Durham, and of Winchester. He is also Archbishop of York and Papal Legate in England, which puts him above even the Archbishop of Canterbury. Who knows, he may one day be Pope! So he is the most powerful churchman. He is also Lord Chancellor, and therefore the most powerful layman!" She paused and regarded them both. "I said," she went on, " 'How fortunate for His Grace that the good Cardinal is devoted only to the King and England. Consider how dangerous it would be if so powerful a man had ambitions of his own.' "

For a long moment Wolsey returned her gaze. Then he turned to Henry. "My Sovereign, I confess your royal favors showered on me daily have been more than I deserve. I can render nothing but my thanks, my prayers, and my unending loyalty."

Henry's ruddy face was bright. He was obviously enjoying the game. "What livings would you shed to prove your loyalty, my good vicar of Hell?" he asked.

Wolsey bowed his head. "Any or all, Sire, at your command," he answered.

Anne clapped her hands together, as though in delight at Wolsey's reply. "And your wealth, my lord?" she said lightly. She turned to Henry. "I believe he is richer even than you, Your Grace! So many livings, so many palaces—"

This was something that Henry had not thought of before.

"I wonder," he said. The royal brow knitted.

"Such vanities mean little to me if I may serve you," Wolsey said with a smile that was slightly forced. "Choose anything I have and it is yours, Sire."

"I will, I will," the King said, his forehead still furrowed. "When I have given it some thought," he added. "Thank you, Nan!"

He reached for another arrow and strung it to his bow.

Anne addressed the Cardinal with mock admiration. "My lord," she said, giving him her most charming smile, "you are as generous as you are great! I shall ask the King to show me your palace at Hampton Court."

The King's arrow flew to its target.

Cromwell watched it with his usual air of detachment.

"Bull's-eye!" he observed, not without irony.

Katherine, looking out from her window, could see the party returning to the palace through the gardens. Her ladies-in-waiting spoke in subdued tones. Two or three were busy embroidering altar-cloths. Another held a lute on which she played chords in a minor key. Through the window Katherine could hear Anne's laughter rising above the voices of Henry and George Boleyn and Weston and Norris. Behind them walked Wolsey and Cromwell, along with the two secretaries and the King's archer. The shooting was over for the day, but the party was not done.

Katherine turned her eyes from the window.

"Come, girl," she called to the lute player. "Play something cheerful. Men prefer women who laugh and are gay."

It was night. Anne sat in the King's chamber. She wore a new gown, richer and more beautiful than any she had ever owned before. The magnificent jewels that hung from her ears and throat were also new.

But the King did not sit with her. He strode like a caged lion up and down the room. His mood was savage, a dangerous one for her, as Anne well knew. Henry was not shouting. It was always safer when he did.

He stopped pacing.

"What more do you want?" he demanded.

"Nothing," she said.

"For your family? For your friends?"

She was silent.

"For yourself?"

"Nothing."

"Liar," he roared. "You've a taste for power. It's very common, Madam. I've seen it many times. But you don't get it for nothing. You pay."

"You ordered me to court. The power is yours, not mine."

He came and stood over her. "I am mad for you. I

dream of you at night. I long for you by day. And you dare to say *I* have the power. I'm no good with any other woman. I think of nothing but you: of you and me playing dog and bitch. Of you and me playing at horse and mare. Of you and me every way there is. I want to fill you up, night after night. I want to fill you with sons."

"Bastards?" she answered. "For they would be bastards."

He moved away from her to control his rage. His back was turned to her. The air quivered between them. "If you say one more word I shall strike you," he said between his teeth. "One more word."

Anne rose.

"Without marriage," she said clearly, "if you and I have sons they will be bastards."

He turned and struck her across the face. She lay sprawled full-length across the floor.

Seventeen

Wolsey lay in bed, reading by candlelight, at Hampton Court. Bess, his fond mistress, comfortable and middle-aged, slept at his side.

There was a sudden hammering on the door.

The Cardinal put down his book. "What is it?" he called.

The voice that came in reply was the Duke of Norfolk's. "Norfolk," he called out roughly. "With a message from the King."

"The Devil take him," muttered the Cardinal. He

Scenes on this and the following pages are from the Hal Wallis production of *Anne of the Thousand Days,* a Universal Picture starring Richard Burton and Genevieve Bujold.

Richard Burton as King Henry VIII.

Genevieve Bujold as Anne Boleyn.

Henry sits unhappily with Queen Katherine of Aragon, as he watches young Anne dancing with her lover.

Henry interrupts the pair to request Anne to teach him the dance.

King Henry conspires with Cardinal Wolsey (Anthony Quayle) to arrange a rendezvous with Anne.

Anne, however, scorns the attentions of the king for her true love.

Queen Katherine (Irene Papas) pleads with Henry not to cast her aside.

Katherine protests Henry's attempts to annul their marriage.

Anne continues to spurn Henry unless she becomes queen.

Cardinal Wolsey and the conniving Cromwell (John Colicos) meet opposition from Sir Thomas More (William Squire).

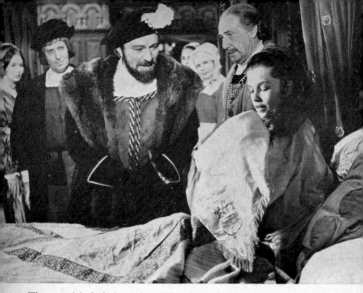

The royal heir is born but Henry's excitement soon turns to anger as he learns the child is a girl.

Later, Queen Anne instructs the baby Elizabeth on queenly carriage.

King Henry's roving eye turns to another, Jane Seymour.

Tragedy strikes on the birth of Anne's second child.

The King demands to know if charges of adultery brought against Queen Anne and a young musician are true.

Condemned to die, Anne of the Thousand Days summons unbelievable courage.

nudged the sleeping woman. "Bess," he said with tenderness.

She awoke and peered amiably at him.

"Begone, Bess," he told her. "Out you go, for form's sake."

She adjusted her nightcap, got out of bed, and, wrapping a gown about her, went out of the room by another door.

"Enter," Wolsey called.

His liveried men opened the doors and Norfolk strode into the bedchamber. "The King commands that you come at once to the palace at Greenwich, Cardinal." Norfolk's dislike of Wolsey was apparent as he spoke.

"Does he, my lord? Is he ill? Is there some urgent danger?"

Norfolk said only, "The boat is waiting," and started to go.

"Norfolk!" Wolsey called suddenly in a sharp voice. He was angry.

The Duke stopped and turned. In a second Wolsey was his bland self again.

"Is the tide with us or against us?" Wolsey asked.

"I leave such details to the boatmen and other riffraff, my lord," Norfolk replied with scorn.

"You may go!" the Cardinal told him.

Norfolk turned on his heel and went out. Bess hurried back into the room to help Wolsey into his robes.

"He sounded as if he hated you, Thomas," she said.

Wolsey's fleshy face was ashen. It was as though in that moment he had a premonition of his fate and his fall from greatness. "They all hate me," he said. "I have administered this kingdom for fifteen years. And if the King ever tires of me, the rest will tear me to pieces."

Bess said gently, "I'll never tire of you, Thomas."

He reached out and patted her warm, broad back. "If only Henry could be as faithful to a woman as I am to you! By my life, Bess, if it were not for my vows of celibacy, I'd marry you."

She gave a soft chuckle as she smoothed the folds of his scarlet robe.

Eighteen

The King roared at Wolsey when he was shown into Henry's chamber at Greenwich.

"What keeps you half the night getting down here when I send for you?"

Henry stood in the middle of the room. Anne sat silent in an Italian chair, her face in the shadows.

"Your Grace's pardon," the Cardinal said humbly. "The tide is flooding."

He looked old and weary, but the King saw none of this. "Now," said Henry. "Now you tell Lady Anne the law of England, my holy lord Cardinal. Is it or is it not true that I can make legitimate whomsoever I choose?"

Wolsey's crafty mind had grasped the situation at once. Or he thought it had. He was sure that the King's final move in the game of getting Anne to bed was to promise to legitimize her children. In the light of Anne's attitude toward him, it would please Wolsey if this worked. He was only too aware, to be sure, of the flaw in Henry's argument, but this he would conceal if he could.

"Most certainly, Your Grace," he said meekly.

"And the documents could be drawn at once?" Henry demanded.

"Within the hour," he assured the King.

Anne spoke up. "Could any child of the King's body be made legitimate, my lord?"

"Yes," the prelate replied.

"And such a child," she pursued, "would be heir to the throne of England?"

"Most certainly."

"Thank you, Thomas," Henry put in. "Take the flooding tide and go home."

Wolsey, with a smile, turned to go.

Anne rose from her chair. "Wait!" she cried.

"Madam?"

"Surely," she said, "such a child would be the heir to the throne *after* Princess Mary—daughter of the King and his rightful Queen?"

The Cardinal hesitated to reply.

Anne held her ground. "Well, my lord?"

"That might be argued," Wolsey hedged.

"No, let us have it clearly." She stood before him like a tree. "Princess Mary is first in line against any son His Grace may father out of wedlock. After Princess Mary comes the Duke of Richmond, his bastard by Bessie Blount. Can you deny that he would inherit if she died?"

"Richmond?" Wolsey considered. "He's a sickly fellow. I doubt if he'll live out the year."

"But he would come first, shall we say? And then my sister Mary's child. Any baseborn son I might have would be younger than Mary's. Her child would come before mine. My entry would be fourth." She held up her hand to prevent Wolsey from breaking in. "We are affectionate sisters, Mary and I. We forgive each other the little things that sisters must forgive. Yet she would rather her son sat on the throne than mine. I'd rather mine than hers. I'd rather have no son than one born a bastard!"

In his blandest voice Wolsey broke in at last. "You may not be capable of a son, Madam. Who knows?"

She retorted in a fury, "I'll give the man that marries me a houseful of lusty sons!"

"Marriage!" Henry bellowed like a gored bull. Then, after a long pause he said deliberately, "If I were free of Katherine—"

Anne turned pale. "You cannot be free of Katherine."

"If I were?" he said, weighting each word with its terrible import.

"It is impossible," Anne said, clenching her hands.

"For the last time," he said, looking into her blenched face with almost agonizing intensity, "if I were free of her, and made you Queen of England— would you marry me?"

Anne stood there, exultant and appalled. Then she said, "Yes. If you make me Queen of England I'll marry you and give you sons. Meanwhile—" she moved toward the door—"meanwhile, I'll go alone to my bed with your gracious leave."

She had gone.

Wolsey smiled. He was quite certain that this too had been another move in a game which would have an inevitable ending.

"Brilliant, Your Grace," he said. "Brilliant!"

Henry regarded him through narrowed eyes. "You think so?"

"Yes. Keep promising her marriage and the siege will soon be over. In a month at most you will have breached her."

"You think I'm lying?"

"If wooing, praise, gifts, and power have failed," he replied smoothly, "then of course you must use a new strategy."

Henry thrust his face into the Cardinal's. "When I go down on my aching knees and pray, good Cardinal, as I do day in and day out, I pray only one thing. I pray to be shown the way to save my kingdom from chaos when I am dead. That prayer has just been answered. I shall remarry and have a son!"

"Divorce?" Wolsey breathed. "Katherine?"

Henry's voice rang with fanatical conviction, with the passion of a man who truly believed his own words. "Annulment! My marriage is cursed and my sons are born dead because I transgressed God's law in marrying my brother's wife. It was incest. And for twenty years I have been punished. I was never married in the eyes of God."

Wolsey, weary, summoned his full strength. "Indeed you were, my Lord, thoroughly married!" he said forcefully. "All the world knows that the Pope granted you a dispensation to marry Katherine when Arthur died."

"Because England and Spain needed each other!"

"No," the Cardinal told him firmly, "because your brother was only a boy of fifteen and there was doubt that he consummated the marriage before he died."

"Fifteen!" Henry shouted. "At fifteen I was rogering maids right left and center. But—at the time of my marriage I believed and the Pope believed and my father chose to believe that Katherine was still virgin. I was deceived. That marriage was consummated. Get me the evidence, Wolsey. Prepare a case for annulment."

"Sire," Wolsey said in alarm, "as your faithful servant, I beg you consider—Katherine is a princess of Spain. Try to annul your marriage and you will gather enormous forces against you: the combination of Spain, Naples, Germany—and the Netherlands, ruled by Katherine's nephew—the Roman Catholic Church all over Europe—your own people, even, who love the Queen."

Stubbornly, Henry said, "I will marry Anne Boleyn. I will have this girl crowned Queen."

"It may mean war," Wolsey pleaded. "Or your death, or the loss of your kingdom."

"I shall make her Queen," Henry said. "If it breaks the earth in two like an apple and flings the halves into the void, I shall make her Queen!"

The Cardinal looked at him steadily. For a moment it seemed to him as though the King were mad. Then, wearily, slowly, he bowed his head.

Nineteen

The Spanish ambassador was in the Queen's chamber at Greenwich. He had come in haste to impart urgent news to her. And now that he had told her, she cast her somber eyes on his long, bearded face.

"No!" she exclaimed. "I don't believe it of him."

"I fear it is true, Madam," he assured her. "I have many sources of information."

"Then it is Wolsey," cried Katherine, "not the King. That butcher's cur Wolsey put it in his mind!"

"Wolsey is preparing the case to take to Rome," he said.

There was a knock on the door then.

"Enter," the Queen called.

One of her ladies-in-waiting sped into the room in a state of agitation. "The King is here. He wishes to see Your Grace."

"I will do all in my power to aid you," the ambassador said quickly to Katherine. "I will send word today to the Emperor Charles."

"Yes," she replied. "And to His Holiness."

The ambassador shrugged cynically. "The Pope bends to the wind, Madam. Your hope is in your nephew, the Emperor." He bent over her hand.

Henry walked into the room.

"Your Grace!" the Spaniard said, with a low bow.

A shadow of displeasure passed over Henry's face. "My lord Ambassador," he said curtly.

The Spaniard took his leave; the lady-in-waiting followed, shutting the door after her. Henry and Katherine were alone.

Katherine dropped into a curtsy. Henry bowed abruptly and then came forward to raise her. She took his hand in both of hers and kissed it fervently. "It delights my heart to see you privately after so many months, my lord."

"Sit, Kate, sit." He helped her into her chair. "Kate, I'll come bluntly to the point." She clasped her hands in the folds of her purple gown to keep them from trembling as she listened. "My conscience is deeply troubled. God tells me our marriage is a sin. Incest will be punished. And we have been punished, you and I, with dead children."

"Our daughter Mary is alive and well, Henry."

70

He ignored her words. "Our marriage must be annulled," he said.

"Then it's true," she burst out. "Wolsey has brought you to this!" Suddenly she was in a flood of bitter tears.

"Kate!" Henry cried. He was deeply troubled. "Kate. It's God's will!"

Katherine shook her head. "My conscience is clear."

"Help me," he implored. "For both our sakes. Support my case to the Pope."

"I am your wife," she answered, holding up her head proudly. "Do you believe that I could ask Pope Clement to tell the world that my father lied, my mother lied—Ferdinand and Isabella, the most Christian princes!—that each lied when they swore my marriage with your brother was never consummated? Your own father signed the paper with them."

"God knows," Henry said stonily, "he lied like a Trojan in season and out."

"Hal," Katherine said, reaching for his indifferent hand. "I've had little happiness in my life. I was a lonely girl brought here from Spain at fifteen to be used for English politics. When Arthur died I was pushed aside and kept here for seven years until I could be used for you. And you I loved. With you I have my only happiness." Her voice broke. "I love you still."

"Then do as I ask," he said.

Her pride flared up again. "I will not betray our daughter," she told him.

"You know the girl's a threat, not a blessing. I must have a son."

She withdrew her hand as though it had been stung. "Get one then," she cried darkly, "on one of your women. But I am your wife, your Queen. Neither you nor the Pope can make my child a bastard." She moved away from him and went toward the window.

"If you defy me," he called after her, "I will have you sent from court and shut away in the country!"

Katherine turned.

"It is you, then, and not Wolsey who really wants this thing."

71

He stood with his feet planted apart, like a willful boy, like an absolute monarch. "I will have it," he said.

"I, too, gave evidence that my marriage to Arthur was never consummated. Did I lie to the Pope all those years ago? Did I lie to God? Did I lie to you, Hal?"

He looked away.

"No," she cried. "I will live and die your wife and your Queen." She was rigid, her arms pressed to her sides, the diamond cross glinting on her breast and the light from the window blazing behind her.

Without a word, Henry swung about and stalked out of her chamber.

Twenty

There was a great massing of scarlet and gold in the courtyard and in the forecourt of Greenwich Palace.

The Cardinal was about to leave for Rome.

Grooms moved among the waiting horses. Wolsey's liveried retainers, his attendant clergy with glinting crosses and flashing symbols of office, and his men-at-arms stood gathered waiting for the signal for departure. Wolsey himself, his portly figure encased in scarlet, his great broad-brimmed hat shadowing his aging face, stood giving his final instructions to a cleric.

"As soon as I reach Rome," he said, "I shall send dispatches back by way of Holland. See that messengers are there."

A lean figure in sober clothes came running toward them across the grass. It was Thomas Cromwell. "My lord," he said, "news has just arrived from Italy that the Emperor Charles, with the Imperial army, is attacking the Papal States."

Wolsey reflected for a moment. "Our impatient King will be glad to hear that," he observed.

"How so?"

Wolsey advanced to the scarlet litter that was waiting for him, Cromwell at his heels. "The Queen is aunt to the Emperor Charles, is she not?" he said thoughtfully.

Cromwell nodded.

"When it comes to a divorce," the prelate went on, "Katherine will look to her nephew for support. He will go to the Pope. Well, Charles is hardly likely to be in the Pope's high favor at the moment, and therefore His Holiness will be more receptive to our Henry's cause."

"So everything is to our advantage," Cromwell put in with a wry smile.

"*Our* advantage? It depends upon how you look at it, Thomas. If I do not obtain the Pope's permission for the divorce, Henry's anger will fall upon me. If the divorce is granted I fear it will not be a good thing for England." Laboriously he got into his litter, easing himself onto the scarlet pillows with an intake of breath.

Cromwell brushed aside the gold-encrusted curtains and leaned in. "Well, Your Eminence," he remarked, "you're damned if you do and damned if you don't."

"You have it in a nutshell, Thomas," Wolsey replied with a dry chuckle. "Farewell!"

Cromwell stood back and watched the magnificent assembly ride away.

From the upper battlements of the palace two other figures watched the procession set out for Rome.

"Not long," said Henry, full of confidence. "Not long to wait now, Nan."

Anne said slowly, "I shall believe it on the day it happens."

They looked down.

Through the bright Thames-side landscape, the great cortege was making its slow portentous way.

Twenty-One

The weeks passed.

Queen Katherine spent most of her time in the chapel, immobile, praying at the altar, tears streaming down her sallow cheeks.

For Henry and Anne and the courtiers, the time was spent in the usual revelries that filled the palace: hunting and sports, feasting and dancing, music and laughter.

The months passed.

The Queen remained at her prayers while the court prepared a masque.

On the night of the masque, the court wore its most splendid attire. Anne wore a new gown, new jewels. The King, in sumptuous brocade and with matchless jewels in his hat, danced behind his mask. The golden mask that Anne held up to shield her face was no less artfully contrived than the King's. When they lowered their masks in the course of the dancing, it was to kiss. Then, masked again, they whirled on through the rout of bounding masquers.

Suddenly a great draft swept through the hall. Through the opened doors came the Cardinal, bent with weariness, his robes stained with the mud and dust of travel.

The dancing stopped as the revelers turned to look

at him. The music faltered and then squeaked into silence.

Silence shrouded the hall.

"Well?" Henry called.

The Cardinal's bulk moved toward him.

"The Spanish Emperor has captured the Vatican," Wolsey said.

The King tossed aside his golden mask. "Captured the Vatican!" he echoed, incredulous.

Wolsey held out his hands. "Rome is sacked. The dead lie in hundreds, unburied in the streets."

The stunned onlookers crossed themselves.

"And the Pope?" Henry demanded.

"Is besieged," Wolsey said.

"Then tell me—"

The Cardinal cut in. "With your gracious permission," he said, "in private."

They left the room, leaving Anne to stand forlorn and alone in the center of the staring courtiers.

Out in the corridor, Henry pushed Wolsey against the wall.

"Well?" he demanded. "Well?"

"The Pope fled from the Vatican to the hill town of Orvieto. I could not reach him. But we exchanged letters."

"Yes?" Henry pursued. "Yes? And the annulment?"

"He refuses to annul your marriage."

Henry clenched his fist. "He cannot refuse."

"He cannot do anything else," the Cardinal replied.

"What are his reasons?"

Wolsey made a small impatient gesture. "His theological reasons are unimportant. The Spanish Emperor has him by the nose. The Pope is not going to offend that Emperor by annulling his aunt's marriage to you!"

A shrill laugh cut through the murk of the corridor. Anne stood just inside the door, her mask held out, pointing to the King.

Henry turned to her. She looked mockingly at him. "Poor Henry!" she said.

His face grew mottled with rage. "He shall, by God Almighty. I say he shall," he bellowed. "And to Hell with the Emperor!"

Twenty-Two

Early the following day, at the royal bidding, Wolsey and Cromwell made their appearance in the King's chamber. With them they brought a cloud of dark-doubleted clerks.

Henry sat at a long table in the center of the room. It was littered with open books, over which the King had been poring.

A huge tome banged down onto the table and Henry's hand struck the open page.

"Incest!" he said.

They gathered around him. Cromwell was already prepared to make notes.

"The case has two parts," the King expounded. "One: the union is contrary to God's law. See the decrees in Leviticus, 'If a man shall take his brother's wife it is an impurity; they shall be childless.'" He rummaged on the table and opened various volumes at markers which had been placed between their pages. "Canon law, see here; Greek scholars and here, Hebrew—here, decrees of Council: all, all are to the point. And the point is that such a marriage is incestuous." He strode over to a standing lectern from which he pulled an enormous book. He slammed the book in front of Wolsey. "Even Aquinas will serve our purpose!" He turned toward an elderly man in a furred cloak who had been standing patiently by. "And the proof we offer? The word of Sir Anthony Wiloughby, who spoke with my brother on the morning following the wedding." He prodded the old man. "Tell them, Wiloughby."

It was only too apparent that Wiloughby was frightened of Henry, and that along with his serious mien he was also inclined to be pedantic and slow of speech.

He cleared his throat. "Prince Arthur came out of his bride's chamber," he began, "in very good cheer. I remember that well, my lords." He cleared his throat again before resuming. "He asked for wine. 'Because,' he said, 'because—' "

Henry, unable to contain his impatience, broke in on the old man's account. " 'Because last night,' he said, 'I was *in* Spain and marriage is a thirsty business.' Ha! And you'll take your oath on it, eh, Wiloughby?" The King indicated a clerk who waited at the foot of the table. "Write it down. Katherine was no virgin. Write it and sign it." Wiloughby, trembling with nervousness, moved to the clerk and began to dictate. Henry turned to Wolsey. "Well, Thomas? Well? What do you think?"

"Yes, yes, Your Grace . . ." Wolsey felt tired. Things were somehow slipping away from him, he felt. He had to play for time. "That is the first part of the case. What is the second?" he asked.

"Ah!" Henry said. "This: the dispensation granted to me by the now dead Pope Julian for my marriage to Katherine was not in itself legal."

For a moment Wolsey glanced at Cromwell. This suggestion was obviously ludicrous. "Yes . . . yes . . ." he murmured. He felt as he spoke that he was treading on eggs. "But, Your Grace, that directly challenges the authority of the Pope."

There was a long pause during which Henry looked steadily at his minister. The royal wind had changed. The King no longer trusted Wolsey.

"Do you oppose me?" Henry asked.

Cromwell's hard eyes were fixed on them both, weighing, measuring, calculating.

"Oppose you?" Wolsey said blandly. "Never, Sire."

Henry pressed his point home. "Do you owe more allegiance to the Pope than to me?" he questioned.

"I am your devoted servant," said Wolsey.

"So you say," the King mused. "So you say."

Suddenly Henry turned on the clerk who was painstakingly scratching away at Wiloughby's dictation. "Must you take a year to record every line of evidence?" he roared. "Wolsey, get me the support of the theologians and the scholars in the universities here and abroad. Send your best agents. Now! Begin now!"

Wolsey bowed and made his way out of the chamber. Without so much as a glance at his departing prelate, Henry went back to the table and flung himself into his chair. "Bring me quires and reams of paper," he commanded, "and a dozen quills. I can present the case better than any of you. And, Cromwell, when I've done, it shall be taken to Orvieto. Exiled or not, the Pope will see my cause is just!"

Cromwell stood by the King's desk. His face was inscrutable. But his sharp attorney's mind was racing.

Twenty-Three

A hard winter journey brought Gardiner and Foxe, the English envoys, to Orvieto, where the Pope had holed in after escaping in disguise from the Castel Sant'Angelo.

Clement VII had begun his career as Giulio de' Medici. He had faithfully served his cousin, Leo X, as chancellor. A handsome man with a quiveringly sensitive face, melting eyes, and a suave, caressing manner, he was not a man who met difficulty face to face. He had preferred always to lie, intrigue, temporize, and play for position rather than to hold his ground and fight. And so now, exiled and defeated, he presented a curious aspect to the ambassadors sent by Henry.

Accompanied by their two secretaries, they were ushered by a papal chamberlain into Clement's chamber. The place was in a state verging on ruin. A few members of the Swiss Guard, unshaven, the worse for wear and in undress uniform, stood about lackadaisically. The very air was shabby. And the Pope himself was in bed. What the English envoys saw was no longer the suave man with compelling eyes about whom they had heard. He was long-bearded now, whey-faced, and suffering from a stomach ailment that affected his disposition and made him short-tempered. It was not easy for the envoys to dissemble and hide their amazement

The chamberlain announced them. "Holy Father. The ambassadors of Henry, by the Grace of God, King of England and Ireland, Defender of the Faith."

The Pope's only companions were Cardinal Campeggio and a secretary, to whom he had been dictating from his bed.

Gardiner and Foxe solemnly began the ritual approach of the three genuflections. Then, in turn, they advanced and kissed the ring.

"Do not mock us with ceremony," Clement told them. "We are a fugitive, in a ruin. The Emperor's troops are everywhere in the land "

Casting a sidelong glance at Campeggio, Clement went on: "We are happy to greet the ambassadors of the English King, our faithful son. We are deeply concerned by the matter on his tender and Christian conscience—"

Two monks came in unceremoniously, bearing food and wine. Clement proceeded to eat and drink, to ease the gnawing in his vitals that was now almost incessant. He spoke while he ate.

"Unhappily," he went on, "you bring your case at a bad time. Our most learned advisors are scattered by the invading Spaniards—"

Gardiner pointed to the documents carried by the two secretaries. "The opinions we have—"

A travel-worn officer in muddy boots burst into the chamber and hurried toward the Pope.

Gardiner raised his voice. "The opinions we have from universities all over Europe, Holy Father—"

He broke off. Clement was not attending him but listening instead to the officer, who was whispering earnestly in his ear.

"The Emperor?" the envoys could hear Clement whispering in return. "How near?"

Gardiner observed to Foxe in an undertone, "Spain, breathing down his neck!"

Foxe asked in a low voice, "Must we go back to tell Henry he can't have his Nan?"

"Not if I can help it!" Gardiner whispered back. He raised his voice doggedly. "Your Holiness, our King cannot outrage his Christian conscience by living in incest any longer. Unless you help him, he will find a way himself to free his bonds!"

Clement, although stripped of his pomp, was still the head of his church, and a man long accustomed to dealing with threats. "As you spoke," he said, his old suavity coming to the fore, "it came to us that the matter *should* be settled in England. We are too far from England to sort truth from falsehood, and too deafened with war. Therefore, we send you our Cardinal Campeggio here, as legate to hear the case." Campeggio moved forward and bowed, and as he did so it was clear that he was crippled with gout. "His decisions shall be ours, and binding as such. And now, farewell."

Clement extended his hand with its ring. The audience was over. The English envoys bowed out, almost knocking over a physician who was on his way in with his bowl to bleed the Pope.

Briskly, the physician rolled up Clement's sleeve.

The Pope waited until the English delegation was out of sight. Then he beckoned Cardinal Campeggio back to his side. "Proceed as slowly as possible," he instructed him. "Pronounce no judgment until our peace is made with the Spanish Emperor." He raised his hand to give Campeggio his blessing, but the physician pulled it down and applied the scalpel.

Clement's blood spurted into the bowl.

Twenty-Four

At Blackfriars, in London, the vast stone hall of the Dominican Charter House was slowly filling up. It was a solemn occasion—one, indeed, of unusual gravity: the holding of a church Court.

In the crowd were courtiers in bright dress, church clerics, Dominican monks in their habits of black and white, chaplains, gentlemen-at-arms. Sir Thomas More arrived and unobtrusively took his place on a bench. Behind him, in a chair, sat John Fisher, the Bishop of Rochester. Behind Bishop Fisher stood John Houghton, the Prior of the Charter House.

Bishop Fisher leaned forward to Sir Thomas More. "More," he said.

Without looking back, More replied, "My lord Bishop?"

"Shall you in your conscience," Fisher inquired quietly, "accept the annulment if the decision is for the King?"

"The Pope has finally answered the King's appeal and has sent Cardinal Campeggio to try this case," More said in a formal tone. "Campeggio speaks for His Holiness. I will accept that."

Bishop Fisher said, "I shall speak against it while I have breath."

"I shall be silent," replied Sir Thomas More, "until I am forced to speak."

For a moment Fisher's grim old face relaxed into a smile.

"Well, I am an old man and have no family. At my age a good death is better than a bad conscience."

As he leaned back in his chair, there was a sudden rush of courtiers to find places. All the King's boon companions had arrived: Smeaton, Norris, Brereton, and Weston were racing for seats. Then another phalanx of noblemen, led by Norfolk in the company of Thomas and Elizabeth Boleyn, moved on down to take their positions in the hall. George Boleyn was also among them. After they had settled themselves, Norfolk turned and spoke to the Boleyns.

"You will be the father and mother, and I the uncle, of a queen next week," he predicted.

"God be praised," Boleyn replied with fervor.

Lady Elizabeth sighed. "I wonder how Anne is thinking?" she said.

Anne, in fact, was not very far away. There was a small robing chamber in the Charter House with a narrow interior window through which the entire proceedings in the great hall could be viewed. Anne had taken her station there.

Henry was in the center of the room with Wolsey. Both King and prelate wore somber expressions, but the King rubbed his hands together confidently.

Anne turned and spoke to him. "Henry, you fool yourself," she said. "I believe the Pope has sent this Cardinal merely as a delaying tactic. He knows the churchmen here will take Katherine's part. With Campeggio as judge, this court won't free you to marry me."

"Out there," Henry replied, with an assured wave of his hand, "are my bishops, my courtiers, and my loyal subjects."

"Campeggio is not your subject," she reminded him.

Wolsey intervened. "But I am," he said. "And, Your Grace, I promise you the verdict." With a bow, he left them and went slowly out toward the great hall.

"You will see, Nan," Henry said. "Wolsey has never let me down yet."

82

But his words did not dispel the troubled shadow on her face.

With Wolsey's appearance, the procession of cardinals had begun in the great hall. The Dominican habits all around them made their scarlet robes glow more vividly. Before them marched their clerics and the bearers of their symbols of office. Wolsey moved like a stately ship in full sail. Campeggio, lean and dark-complexioned, limped on his gouty leg and used a black stick.

Thomas More leaned backward and whispered to Fisher, "Perhaps the Reverend Cardinal's limp explains the delay. He walked from Rome."

Fisher replied mildly, "A reluctance to do injustice is a more suitable explanation, Sir Thomas."

There was a restless murmur as the two cardinals settled down in their thrones. Wolsey raised his hand in signal to the usher.

"Pray silence for His Eminence the Lord Cardinal of York!" the usher called out. His voice echoed in the high rafters.

The Charter House quieted down. All eyes were fixed on Wolsey.

"Our commission from Rome having been publicly read, this enquiry will now proceed," Wolsey's voice droned. He nodded to the usher.

"Henry, King of England," the usher called out, "come into Court."

Henry appeared alone and strode to the throne that had been set up for him, with the royal coat of arms above it.

"Here, my lords."

He sat. The chair for the Queen was level with his but across from him and unoccupied. Once again Wolsey nodded to the usher.

"Katherine, Queen of England, come into Court," the stentor called.

They waited, but the Queen did not appear. The whole Charter House stirred as the audience took in the fact that Katherine had not come to Blackfriars. The speculative buzz abated into complete silence as all eyes turned to look at Henry.

The King suddenly rose to his feet.

"On, on," he shouted.

Wolsey turned to Campeggio. The Italian Cardinal's face was grim, as stony as his native travertine. "What can I do," he asked quietly of Wolsey, "if the Queen will not appear?"

"My lord Cardinal!" Wolsey said urgently.

"Ecco!" Campeggio muttered to himself. He leaned back in his throne. "The King may proceed," he said loudly.

Henry spoke gravely and with assurance. "I have come to this court not because I wish to discard a wife but because such grave doubts are cast upon my marriage and such grave fears fill my conscience. Is it God's will that sons born of the Queen are dead, or is it God's displeasure? Tormented, and in despair of male issue, I have sought without bias for three years to find if my marriage stands within God's law. Or might I take another wife because the first is unlawful? I do not seek another wife for carnal pleasure——"

The Duke of Norfolk raised his hand to his mouth and permitted himself to smile.

"Nor," Henry went on, "for any displeasure of the Queen's person or age." He paused. "This court will try the validity of my marriage. The bishops assembled here have all signed this document"——he held up a scroll for all to see——"declaring that the marriage is in doubt and must be resolved by trial."

"That is the truth, if it please Your Eminence," Wolsey averred, turning toward Campeggio.

Bishop Fisher rose from his chair. "No, sir. That is not the truth," he said in a firm clear voice.

A reaction of shock ran around the Court.

"I do not give my consent," Fisher said.

"No!" cried Henry. He unrolled the scroll. "Here——'John Fisher, Bishop of Rochester'——your own hand and seal."

Fisher replied calmly, "That is not my hand or seal."

"Wolsey!" Henry roared.

Wolsey leaned forward. "Your memory is failing with age, Bishop," he said in a bland even tone. "We

84

argued, and in the end you agreed that I should sign for you and affix your seal."

Fisher shook his head. "My lord, there is nothing more untrue. I told you I would never support this cause."

An air of disapproval filled the Court. Fisher, however, stood silent, holding his ground.

"Well, well," said the King bluffly. "You are only one man. Continue. Hear the witness, my lord Cardinal, who spoke with my brother on the morning he came from the bridal chamber."

"Sir Anthony Wiloughby. Come into Court!" the usher cried.

More, Fisher and John Houghton, the Prior of the Charter House, had their heads together. "Get a message to the Queen, More," the Prior urged. "She should be here! She'll let her case go by default—"

In reply, More only shook his head hopelessly. Even as he did so, however, there was a crash of doors at the end of the great hall, and a stir throughout the entire Court. More turned his head. "God help her," he said. "Here she is."

There, indeed, was the Queen, standing at the doors with her ladies behind her.

There was a flicker in Campeggio's dark eyes as he called out, "I will hear the Queen."

Alone, in her stiff gown cut in the austere Spanish style, Katherine went forward to face the two cardinals. She bowed first to the heavy cross which the crossbearer raised before her. She crossed herself. Henry had flung himself onto his throne where he sat half-turned from her, beetling. Then, suddenly, Katherine turned not to her own throne but to Henry's. She fell on her knees at his feet. She took his hand and kissed it.

Anne, staring intently through the narrow window of the robing room, clenched her hands, digging her nails into her palms. She would as gladly have dug them into Katherine's sallow cheeks.

"The Court!" Henry said coldly, drawing his hand away. "Address the Court, Madam."

She clung to his hand and would not release it. "Sir,

I beseech you, for all the love that has been between us, let me have justice and right. I am a poor woman and a stranger born outside this kingdom, and I ask pity and compassion of you. For more than twenty years I have been your true wife. I have been humble and obedient. I have born you seven children, and to my great sadness six have died through no fault of mine. Tell me, my lord, how I have offended you?" Henry wrested his hand from her grasp at last. "As God is my judge," she cried, her voice hoarse with passion and entreaty, "I was a true maid when you first had me. This you know to be true."

No one in the vast chamber stirred. More and Fisher exchanged glances. Campeggio leaned forward on his stick, his lean, intent Latin face not leaving hers for an instant.

"Sire," Katherine resumed tearfully, "you do me a grave wrong to bring me before a court. This Court cannot be impartial. Except for the good Cardinal Campeggio, they are all your subjects and dare not disobey your will or intent." She rose to her feet. "I will only be heard in Rome. I appeal to Rome. I appeal against all judges here. To Rome and to God I commit my cause."

She made a deep curtsy to the King and moved toward the doors.

"Katherine!" the King called after her.

It was as though she had not heard his voice.

"Katherine!" he called again.

The doors swung closed behind her.

Henry turned to the Court in a fury. "Proceed!" he thundered.

But now it was Campeggio who rose from his seat.

"I adjourn this Court," he announced quietly.

For a moment the hall was in a state of uproar.

Then the King, in a rage, strode from his throne and out of the Court, his velvet cloak swinging from his shoulders like a dark cloud.

In the robing room, Anne turned from the window. It was well that there was no one to hear her shrill laughter, for it had an ugly sound.

Twenty-Five

The King raged all the way back to his palace at Greenwich.

Once there, he sent word to the two cardinals that they were to come to him.

And when Wolsey and Campeggio came to him he went on raging.

Thomas Cromwell came with them. He remained in the background, pressed against the tapestried wall, inconspicuous as a shadow in the King's chamber. Anne Boleyn was also present in the room. She too stood in the background while Henry paced back and forth, fulminating at the scarlet churchmen.

"You have the power, and I say you shall use it!" he concluded on a threatening note.

Campeggio said placatingly, "Power to hear the case, Your Grace—"

"You've heard it," Henry broke in. "Hours of it!"

"From your own witnesses," the Italian cardinal went on, outwardly unruffled. "The Queen says no court in England can be impartial. She appeals directly to Rome."

"You are Rome come to England, my lord!" Henry reminded him.

Campeggio shrugged his shoulders. *"Beh,"* he exclaimed, "my hands are tied. The trial is adjourned for the Queen's appeal."

"To the Pope," Henry shouted, "who fears the Queen's nephew more than he loves the justice of God!"

Campeggio started up from his seat. His leathery old

face twitched. "Your Grace could be excommunicated—"

Henry's anger swelled. It filled the room. "Get out. Limp back to Rome. Tell His Holiness I will have the marriage annulled. Go."

In silence, Campeggio left.

Henry's eyes turned to Wolsey.

Wolsey hesitated to reply to the question in them. He was desperate.

"Well, my lord Cardinal," Anne called mockingly, "so much for your boastful promises!"

"Your Grace, forgive me . . ." Wolsey threw himself prostrate on the floor at Henry's feet. "Forgive me," he murmured brokenly.

There was a pause before Henry spoke. When he did, there was no forgiveness in his voice. "Go to the Queen," he said with contempt. "Banish her from court. House her at your own expense in some remote place."

Wolsey laboriously got to his feet. No one reached to help him. "Yes, Your Grace."

"And yourself, Wolsey." The air crackled with Henry's scorn. "Remove yourself from my sight. You are unfit for office. Render up the great seal. And hide, Wolsey, from my anger. Go now."

Surrounded by terrible silence, Wolsey moved heavily toward the door.

"I do not forgive you," Henry called after him. "I spare you for your past services."

Wolsey went through the door. It closed behind him.

Cromwell remained in his place. He was as still as a statue. Only his eyes moved, calculating. He was prepared to risk everything.

"Well, what do you want?" Henry demanded. "Has the Cardinal forgotten something?"

Cromwell remained silent. He had made the decision but still he did not dare.

"The business of the day is over, lawyer!" the King told him.

Cromwell took the first step forward. "Forgive me, Your Grace. I am a lawyer who has read the law."

88

"So?"

"I am not a fanatic, not a madman, Your Grace. All my life I have been an earnest student at the inns of court. I have read the laws of England, something which few seem to have bothered to do."

The King waited impatiently.

Cromwell took another step closer to the King. "There is a law of this land that says it is treason to acknowledge any higher authority than the will of the King. It is, I take it, the will of the King that he shall divorce the Queen and marry Lady Anne."

Henry nodded. "It is!"

"Then the church in England must grant the King a divorce if he wishes it. To maintain that the Pope may govern the King in such a matter—or in any matter—is traitorous and punishable by death. There is such a law, Your Grace. It is called the law of *praemunire.*"

"I have always been a defender of the faith. And of the church. That is my greatest strength with my people," Henry insisted. "I can't change there."

Cromwell took a breath and came forward so that he was face to face with the King. "Allow me to say a word on that subject, Your Grace. As matters stand you are but half a king. We are only half-subject to you. If you were truly King in England, could a foreign prelate call you to account? England is only half-free. You are only half-free. What the King of England wants he should have, without hindrance from abroad."

"True," Anne cried, running forward to Henry. "It is true. Today you were subject to the ruling of a foreign cardinal. I saw you, the King of England, bow to him. I heard you *plead* your cause to him."

Henry paused, reflecting.

"That would mean excommunication. It would mean a complete break with Rome."

Cromwell was ready. "To bring about all these things you wish," he said eagerly, "the King has only to appoint a new primate of the church in England who would legalize his divorce and a new marriage."

It was now the King's mind that went racing. "And

the penalty for all those good men who could not stomach your law, Master Cromwell?"

"The penalty for treason," Cromwell replied evenly, "has always been death, Your Grace."

Henry nodded. "You may go," he said dryly.

Cromwell did not go, however. "There is something else, Your Grace."

"Well?"

"Cardinal Wolsey, through skillful manipulation, has seen to it that the monasteries of England are richer than the gold mines of the New World. Quarrel with Rome, set yourself at the head of the English church, and these riches are yours. At one stroke you would obtain your divorce and make yourself the wealthiest monarch in Europe!"

For the first time the King regarded him closely.

"You are a man without scruple, Master Cromwell," he observed.

"Entirely without scruple, Sire," the lawyer replied. He smiled grimly. "I learned my trade, as you know, under Cardinal Wolsey."

"You are dismissed," the King told him. "But I shall be able to find you if I need you?"

"Yes, Your Grace."

He bowed out of the room.

It was not until the door of the King's chamber closed behind him that he broke out into a terrible sweat. His face twisted into a grimace of triumph. He had risked everything—and he had won.

Anne and Henry looked at each other after Cromwell left them. There was a pause. Then Anne spoke. "Do you think he tells the truth?" she asked.

"There would be little point in his girding up his courage and speaking to us unless he told the truth."

"Is there such a law?"

Henry shrugged. "I've never heard of it, but he convinces me there is."

"The Cardinal seems to have stolen an immense amount of money."

"Doubtless," Henry replied. He stood pondering. "Doubtless he stole more than I knew, though I'm not exactly innocent in the matter. We sometimes went halves."

"Are you also a pupil of the Cardinal's?"

Henry said, "I am the son of Henry the Seventh. I studied under a real master—my father. Whatever crookedness was lacking in the world when my father was born, he invented before he left it. No other king of our island ever stole so widely, so successfully, so secretly—or died so rich. But the central principle he taught me was this: always keep the church on your side."

"You have the church on your one side," she told him, "and you have me on the other."

"Yes," he admitted. "The choice is now clear. If I set myself up as head of the church in England I make you my queen; I make myself wealthy beyond any other monarch in Europe. But I then make the church my enemy. I am then excommunicated." He paused and stared ahead of him. "Everlasting damnation: in this life no son of the church must speak with me, feed me, or shelter me; and when dead my body must lie without burial—and my soul shall be cast into Hell forever."

A heavy silence lay between them.

After a while Anne said softly, "If Parliament passes such a law," she asked, "you could—'legally'—defy Rome?"

Henry spoke his thoughts aloud: "Suppose I set out to make myself head of the church. I shall be opposed by many who are now my friends. They will be guilty of treason and I shall have to kill them. Those whom I like best—those who have some integrity of mind— will speak first against me. They must die. Parliament and the nation can then be bludgeoned into silence— but a lot of blood will run before they're quiet. The altar at St. Paul's will stand ankle-deep in blood. The shopkeepers will mop blood from their floors . . . But it must be done if we're to marry." He stretched out his hands in a gesture of resignation. "Well, so be it."

"Must so many die?" asked Anne.

"Many must die. Most of my people will hate me— and even more will hate you. Yes, I can make my Nan

Queen, but we must consider the price: in how much we dare be hated. Are we willing to pay it?"

"We?" she repeated. "This is your game, and you know it. I am but a pawn in it."

He suddenly grasped her shoulders and shook her.

"Yes," he cried, "I will do it—if I do it—for you, for your love! If only you could love me with your whole heart!"

He let go of her and turned his face away. She moved toward him and put out her hand, touching his arm.

"But the price is too high," she reminded him gently.

"You're new to this work, Anne. You don't know quite what it means to see the blood run." He shut his eyes. "If you knew, I wonder if you'd still wish it?"

"And you love me—not quite enough," she said, looking away.

He took her hand.

"You shall see," he said.

Twenty-Six

Henry Tudor prayed. He stayed for a long time on his knees before the altar in the chapel at Greenwich, keeping vigil in the night.

"Heavenly Father," he beseeched, "what I set out to do is not for myself, as You know, but for the future safety of my realm and for the great glory of Your name. Should I weaken in my resolve, remember I am but a man. Give me Your divine strength for my intended journey, and—" His eyes rose to the vaulted ceiling. "And resolve my doubts," he concluded. He crossed himself firmly, heaved himself to his feet, and, having rested his case with the Almighty, strode out of the chapel and went to bed.

Twenty-Seven

The main hall of the palace at Greenwich was serving as the council chamber. The council had assembled at the King's bidding, and were now watching Henry solemnly as he addressed them. In the forefront were the Duke of Norfolk, Thomas Boleyn, Bishop Fisher, and the Lord Chancellor of England—Sir Thomas More, who had succeeded Wolsey in the office. Cromwell was at the King's elbow. These were the principal members of the council.

"I intend to bring before Parliament matters which have caused us great concern," Henry told them. "I have been greatly alarmed by the increasing influence and power in our realm of the church as directed by Rome. Already the church is the largest land-owner in our country. The church has continued to drain enormous profits of wealth from my subjects through taxes and fees. Part of these funds are being sent regularly to Rome, and a substantial part finds its way into the pockets of certain cardinals, bishops, and priests. Not content alone with the misappropriation of property and money, Rome now seeks to interfere with the laws and statutes of this realm and the King's prerogatives relating to the succession of the throne. For all of these reasons and others, well-known to you, we must free ourselves from the intervention, influence, and direction of the See of Rome."

There was a general chorus of whispering around the table, along with a few scattered cries of approval.

Henry stretched out a hand to Cromwell, who gave him two documents. Henry held up the first. "Item: the oath of allegiance to the King of England sworn by all of you." In his other hand, he held up the second paper. "Item: the oath of allegiance to the Pope in Rome, sworn by the clergy. Question: whom do the clergy of England serve—Pope or King?"

Those in the council who were members of the clergy exchanged glances of alarm and discomfiture, while Norfolk and his companions smiled with gloating pleasure.

Henry reached for still another document from Cromwell. "Item: a law of this realm concerning treason," he called out. He paused. Then, slowly, weighing his words, he went on. "Question: are the clergy of this realm, in particular the bishops, guilty of treason?"

A deathly quiet reigned in the council hall.

Henry handed all the documents back to Cromwell.

"Cardinal Wolsey, the greatest churchman in this last is cast down," the King continued. "Any priest or bishop who does not first serve the King will follow him." He made a sign to Cromwell who laid on the table the bill that had been prepared to go before Parliament. "Parliament will be summoned," he announced, "for the enactment of this bill called the Act of Supremacy, whereunder the King is declared to be supreme in all matters touching the welfare of his subjects, both temporal and spiritual."

Sir Thomas More and Bishop Fisher sought each other's eyes.

Bishop Fisher rose to speak.

"My lord Bishop, keep silent!" Henry shouted. "There is only one question that I will put to the council. No other may be discussed. The question to you is this: does any lord here, spiritual or temporal, deny the right of Parliament to enact this bill and make it the law of England—if Parliament should so choose?" He paused and cast his eyes around the council table. On one side of it, the black-and-white-robed clergy sat apprehensive and glum; on the other, the velvet-caparisoned courtiers were unable to conceal their delight.

Henry turned his glance on More.

"Sir Thomas?"

"I do not deny the right of Parliament to enact laws," Sir Thomas More replied soberly.

"Ha!" the King crowed. "Next business, Cromwell."

Cromwell shuffled his papers officiously. "The next business, Your Grace, is the business of your divorce."

"Advise me," commanded Henry.

"It was in error that Cardinal Wolsey appealed to the Pope," Cromwell proceeded in a dry bureaucratic tone. "It was in error that the opinion was sought from foreign theologians. When Parliament passes the Act of Supremacy you will be first under God, and a court of English bishops will be empowered to grant your divorce."

"I am grateful for your counsel. Next!"

Sir Thomas More had risen.

"More?" The King once more turned his attention to the Chancellor.

"Cardinal Wolsey sends you his humble duty," More said in a quiet voice.

There was a stir on both sides of the council.

"And he begs," More went on, "that you will accept, as a gift, his palace at Hampton Court."

Henry said, steely-eyed, "And?"

"And he further begs," More continued, "that he may be allowed to serve you again, Sire, although he is now ill and perhaps has not long to live."

Henry paused for a moment before replying. He looked significantly at Bishop Fisher. Then he said, "Sick men should rest, and be glad to be left in peace."

The Duke of Norfolk's mouth curved in a smile of triumph.

"We accept the gift," Henry said.

Norfolk laughed outright.

The session of the council was ended. Henry left the hall with Norfolk and Boleyn and a number of other courtiers in his train. The rest of the council remained talking among themselves. They stood apart as Sir

Thomas More moved over to speak to Thomas Cromwell.

"Master Cromwell," More said in a low, even voice.

"My lord Chancellor."

"I regret, Master Cromwell," More told him mildly, "that you did not heed my advice."

Cromwell looked at him, surprised.

"Advice? Concerning what?"

"You have, I believe, told the King not what he ought to do, but what he can do; and now no man in the world can hold him."

"The King's power must be complete," the lawyer replied coldly.

"And your own?"

Cromwell gave him a frosty smile. "To serve his," he said.

Sir Thomas More touched the heavy chain of office that hung about his neck. "After today," he said, "I fear I must resign mine."

There was a slight pause. Cromwell continued to smile. "Every man to the Devil in his own way," he answered.

More merely smiled in return.

Cromwell moved off. The Chancellor was left there alone. His eyes were clear. He knew what the future held for him.

Twenty-Eight

Wolsey sat at his desk in his working-room at Hampton Court.

He was alone, his writing hand slowly moving over

a document. His fall from power and grace had left him a broken old man, heavy with dropsy and crippled with arthritis. The stick without which he could no longer move leaned against his chair.

At the sound of laughter from beyond the door the Cardinal glanced up. He recognized the voice of Anne Boleyn rising gaily above the laughter.

And then the door was flung open and Cromwell bowed Henry and Anne into the room. They had all three been riding, and their clothes bore the signs of it. Their voices were high, their faces cheerful.

They stopped at the sight of Wolsey.

"Forgive me, Your Grace," Wolsey said. "I had meant to be gone. I can neither kneel nor bow, I fear. Your hand, Thomas, to get me to my feet."

Cromwell helped the Cardinal rise. Wolsey leaned heavily on his stick.

"It is the habit of a lifetime," Wolsey explained wryly, "to see to it myself that the inventory is complete, and all the keys are ready and labeled for you."

A pang of true concern touched the King. "I am sorry to see you ill," he said.

Wolsey raised his hand in a gentle protest. "No, no, Sire. Your Grace has taken from my shoulders a load that would sink a navy. Now I'll sign the inventory and go. Is it for you, Mistress Anne, the palace?"

"Yes," she replied, her head high.

He nodded. "Yes," he said, "it is much too beautiful for an old man. It needs youth in it." He affixed his signature to the document on the table. It was the inventory. "Take it," he said.

Anne looked him in the eye. "I have been your enemy," she said slowly, "but I cannot take it from you."

He said, "Then I'll leave it. A leggy girl—and a half-grown steer," he added in a low musing voice.

"What?" Henry said.

Wolsey shook his head, as though to erase from the air the words he had spoken. "Your Grace," he said, "some friends of yours are waiting to see you: More, Fisher, and Prior John Houghton. It seemed urgent."

Henry exchanged a look with Cromwell.

"Urgent for them!" snapped the King. "Let them come in."

"I'll tell them as I leave," Wolsey said. Laboriously, he made his way toward the door. Halfway across the room he paused and pressed his hand against his leg. "The joints!" he murmured to himself. In silence he went to the door, opened it, and let it swing closed behind him.

For a brief moment Henry felt a twinge of guilt. "He's aged!" he exclaimed. Then his mood changed. "The country air will be good for him at Esher," he said.

In the hall, Bishop Fisher and Prior Houghton bowed coolly to the Cardinal as he came toward them, moving slowly on his stick. Only More wore a friendly mien.

"The King will see you," Wolsey told them.

The Bishop and the Prior went past him and through the door. As Sir Thomas More made to follow them, Wolsey reached out and grasped his sleeve, stopping him.

"Take heed, Sir Thomas," he said in a low voice. "The King's passion for the lady is blind to all reason and past service."

More remained silent. Then, looking at Wolsey for a moment, he said gravely, "My lord, for your wisdom I am sorry to see you go."

"Sir Thomas," Wolsey began. Then his voice broke at the kindness in More's words. "The King has gone beyond me. I'm lost forever." More was silent. Wolsey bit his lip and recovered. "Do not neglect the King," Wolsey told him, "but look to your own safety."

More replied with a small smile. "It happens, my good lord, that I have been unwell lately. Therefore I must give up my office, leave the court, and go home. There I will speak of nothing but domestic affairs."

Wolsey slowly made the sign of the cross over him. "Well," he said softly, "God be with you."

More left to join the others. For a moment Wolsey was alone. For the last time he looked around at his home, at the beauty and the splendor he had created and was now leaving.

Then he gathered his painful limbs and limped away.

Bishop Fisher and Prior Houghton stood facing the King in the room that had lately been the Cardinal's office. More waited in the background, behind his friends. Cromwell remained in his place at the King's elbow, while Anne watched from the shadows behind them.

Bishop Fisher was speaking. His lean face, with the sun streaming onto it from the windows, seemed worn and old. "I was your father's confessor," he reminded Henry. "I watched you take your first steps and I have known you all your life. I have written against the divorce, preached against it, and opposed it in court. I come now to beg you—" he kneeled creakily—"on my knees, for the sake of your immortal soul, to return to the church, to submit to the Pope, to bring your rightful Queen back to court."

"I think not, old man," the King replied coldly.

Fisher looked steadily at the King. Then he rose. "I have also watched you govern for many years, King Henry. You are very shrewd in judging what you dare do. It is as if you had an extra sense, the King's finger so to speak, and you keep it on the pulse of your subjects."

"Yes, Bishop," Henry said with a saturnine smile. "The people will go with me."

"Tell me why?" Fisher asked. His grim wrinkled face was turned on Henry's, waiting for his reply.

"Because, old man, they want to be free of Rome. They'll take me rather than some foreigner overseas. This wasn't true ten years ago. It is only beginning to be true now." The King and the Bishop faced each other. It was a deadlock. Neither the man of God nor the man of power would lower his eyes. "Must you still refuse to sign?" Henry asked at last.

Fisher answered, "I have no King's finger. I cannot accept your guidance in spiritual matters. I must follow my own conscience. I cannot sign."

Henry turned to Houghton.

"And you, Prior John?"

Houghton too looked weary, and his years showed on his face. "The Act of Supremacy was passed, Your Grace," he said slowly. "But now we are asked to swear an oath of fealty to you as spiritual head of the church."

"It is Pope or King," Henry said unyieldingly. "One or the other."

Houghton's hooded eyes were steady. "For me," he said, "it must be the Pope."

"Then—though I am sorry to lose old friends—you will be guilty of treason," Henry told him, "and you will die for it."

"There are hundreds of my order who in good conscience cannot take this oath," the Prior said evenly. "Must they all die?"

"If they wish to die, they may. If they insist, they will. My cause is just. I am denied it by a Pope who is the puppet of the Emperor of Spain." The King's voice rang out resolutely: "There must be a divorce, a new queen, a male heir. When the English church is cut adrift from Rome, it must anchor to something. I see no anchor but the King. I had to choose, and so must the clergy." He turned now to More. "Sir Thomas?"

"I have come to say good-bye, Your Grace," More said in his quiet unruffled way. "I gave up my office today as you graciously permitted."

The King paused before saying, "Yes! And when the day comes for you to choose, Sir Thomas? Will you take the oath?"

"I shall read the document with care and hope that my conscience will permit me to sign, Your Grace."

For a long moment Henry looked into the face of the man who was no longer his chancellor.

"Good-bye, Thomas," he said.

Sir Thomas More bowed and went to the door.

Henry advanced toward Fisher and Houghton. He addressed them gravely. "Good-bye, my lord. Good-bye, Prior John. You move away from this world of your own free will, and I am sad for it."

"Your Grace," Bishop Fisher responded with a wry smile, "it will go on without us."

He watched them go. Cromwell too took his leave.

Henry and Anne were alone.

"And that," Henry said thoughtfully, running his hand through his beard, "answers the last of them that dare speak. The rest will die silent." He turned to Anne. "I think there has never been in all this world a king who gave so much to find his way to the heart of the woman he loved. I have fought and chopped and hacked and stabbed my path through the jungle of laws and events and churchly rules—and the flesh of friends—to come to this day." His small mouth twisted into a bitter line. "But not once, not once have you said, 'I love you.' Surely now—surely my Nan will say it now?"

She glanced down at the floor, and then raised her glance to meet his. "Yes," she said. "I do love you."

"So. Then that's not it. That's not what I wanted," he told her.

"What did you want, my lord?"

He held up his empty hands. "I don't know," he replied. "Only—I still don't have you. Nan, did someone say to you—sometime—'Never be all his, never melt to him, never forget to hate him at least a little, otherwise you'll lose him'?"

"I've said it myself."

"Do you say it now?"

"Yes."

"I see," he said dully. "That's what I feel." His voice rose. "Keep your heart then! Preserve your special chastity. I am too old to suffer these pangs of love and longing like a stupid boy; writing desperate poems to the cold-hearted bitch I love and tearing them up; pacing my room night after night, unable to sleep. Sons you have promised me when you are Queen. And sons I will have. Sons without love, if I must. Enjoy your palace. I will not come near you again until the day we marry."

He turned swiftly on his heel and went away.

Anne looked after him.

Suddenly she called out: "Hal!"

He stopped and turned. She ran to him. Falling on her knees, she seized his hand and covered it with passionate kisses.

"I do love you!" she cried. "Oh, Harry, I love you with all my heart!"

"Is this true?" he asked sternly.

Anne rose.

"Take me now," she said. "Make love to me."

They clutched at each other.

"I want to be yours only," she whispered.

"I have been yours—for a long time," he said in a throaty voice. He kissed her fiercely. "And for the first time," he told her, exulting, "you are mine too!"

Twenty-Nine

They bedded happily in Wolsey's great bedroom, with the Cardinal's coat of arms glimmering from the tapestry over their tousled heads.

When the first tumult was over and they lay back, tender and contented in each other's arms, Anne said gently, "Those men who were to die, Henry—let them live."

"It was done for you," he reminded her.

She pressed closer to his chest. "Let them swear or not swear to the Act of Supremacy as they like. I no longer care about the divorce." She placed her face shyly against his naked flesh. "I'm deep in love with one that I hated," she confessed.

"Can it be true after these long years?" he murmured into her hair. He held his hand under her chin and gently raised her face to his. He kissed her. "God be praised, Nan, I do love you."

"And our love will make a son that will rule the world!"

"A son! Nan, with that and your love I can be the king I have wished to be: just, generous, wise, and merciful. So, I will kill no men for your sake." His arm tensed, and his eyes shone brightly in the candlelight. "It's like a new age, wildfire in the air and in the blood!"

His pulse raced. The wildfire tore through him. Then they were both caught up again in its consuming blaze.

The Cardinal's coat of arms flickered as the candles guttered. In the changing light it remained there, now a bright benison, now a shadowy curse.

Thirty

Anne Boleyn's demeanor had altered. Now that her haughty, arrogant, holding-off attitude toward the King had changed, it was a radiant young woman that the courtiers beheld: a true rose for Henry Tudor. And wherever the King went, Anne was not far from his side.

One sunny morning in early spring Anne walked alone, singing to herself, in the gardens of the palace at Greenwich. Her color was high, her step light, and her heart like a bird's. Her thoughts were as gay as the bright new flowers that bordered her path.

Still singing, she turned a corner.

A man's figure was hurrying along the path in her direction. He stopped dead when he caught sight of her. After a second he made a low court bow.

"Harry!" Anne cried. For it was Harry Percy, now Earl of Northumberland. The years—how many had passed since they had last met: four? five? more?—had altered him not a little. He seemed older, coarser-cut than she remembered him.

He said, rather formally, "The King sent for me to meet him here."

"Here?" she asked. "Strange! Perhaps," she said speculatively, "he is jealous and is testing my faithfulness by bringing us together!"

"Perhaps," Northumberland repeated, with the ghost of a smile. "Has he reason to be jealous?"

"No. Never!" she cried.

"Well," he said, his thin smile turning to an ironic grin, "you are his concubine and I have a hag for a wife, and now I am to arrest Wolsey who began it all. Cold comfort."

"Arrest him? He is old and sick," she protested.

"I thought it was your doing," he told her bluntly.

She shook her head. "No," she said. "I am past hating him."

"He had been intriguing with Rome. Your uncle Norfolk has caught him out, and now I am chosen to execute the warrant," Percy informed her.

There was a sound of voices nearby. They looked up.

Henry was approaching with Cromwell.

Percy drew himself up. "I am glad to see you well, Madam," he said with great formality.

"And I you, Sire."

Percy turned and hurried toward the King. Anne saw Henry gesture to Cromwell, and then Cromwell spoke to Percy and handed over the warrant. But Henry did not linger. He hastened over to join Anne. He kissed her hand, then her mouth. In his eyes glinted the jealousy of all rakes who, finally, are caught in the meshes of their own passion.

"Well," he exclaimed. His eyelids were slits. "There was your first love, Anne. There was the one you hated me for. Did your heart race?"

She looked into his contorted face with complete confidence. "No," she said affectionately, "you great royal fool!"

Henry laughed.

"I am a happy man," he said.

"And I, my great King," she answered, "I am with child!"

Henry stared at her, stunned. Then a great gust of delighted laughter burst from him. He lifted Anne into his arms and swung her around and around. The spring morning, the green hedges, the small bright flowers, the gentle sky all swept dizzily past her glad eyes.

Thirty-One

They were married hastily and by night in the Chapel at Whitehall.

Thomas Boleyn, his son George and his brother-in-law, Norfolk, attended the King. Henry strode up and down the aisle with unconcealed impatience. The priest who had been summoned from his bed to perform the ceremony was old and extremely worried. His fingers fumbled as he put on his white stole, and he managed to let his prayer book fall several times.

At last the door opened and Anne appeared, accompanied by her mother, Lady Elizabeth. The women were cloaked. Anne's face was eager. Her eyes shone: not with the triumph that could be discerned on the faces of Norfolk and her parents, but with happiness.

"Begin," Henry commanded. "Begin!"

The priest was half out of his wits with age and his fear of incurring the King's displeasure. "Yes, yes," he stammered. "I mean, Your Grace, the door must be open. That is to say, for legality, witnesses are——"

"Here they are," Henry cut in brusquely. He beckoned forward the two Boleyns and Norfolk. "Now on, man."

"At once, Your Grace." He fumbled again, this time to find the page in his prayer book. "Henry, wilt thou take Anne here present to thy lawful wife according to the rites of our Holy Mother Church?"

"I will!" Henry's voice boomed out.

"Anne, wilt thou take Henry here present to thy lawful husband according to the rites of our Holy Mother Church?"

"I will."

The priest prompted: "I, Henry, take thee, Anne——"

"I, Henry, take thee, Anne——" the King repeated after him.

"——To my wedded wife." He dropped the book again and fumbled for it in his robes. "To my wedded——"

"To my wedded wife," Henry burst in. He raced on, saying the words at a cracking rate, "To have and to hold from this day forward for better, for worse, for richer, for poorer, in sickness and in health, till death us do part——"

The priest caught up with him. "——Us do part, and thereto——"

"And thereto I plight thee my troth," Henry concluded. "And after that, Nan my girl, you shall have bells and a crowning."

Norfolk, in the background, put his lips close to Boleyn's ear. "It's the new fashion," he whispered. "Marry the one before you've divorced the other!"

"Please God," Boleyn whispered back, "he doesn't tire of her before the divorce. If he does, he'll plead bigamy."

"Amen," Norfolk intoned.

The royal wedding was over.

Thirty-Two

The Spanish ambassador was galloping along the track that led to Katherine's country manor of exile. His brows beetled as the house itself came into view: it was a dismal place, long neglected, standing in grounds not well tended. It was no place, he thought angrily, to shelter a daughter of Ferdinand and Isabella of Spain, or a queen of England.

He rode up to the door, dismounted, and hammered on the portal. A groom appeared and took his horse's bridle.

The room in which Queen Katherine received him was furnished barely. A large crucifix of ornate Spanish workmanship was all that hung on the austere walls.

The Queen's eyes glowed balefully in her drawn face as she listened to the ambassador's news. "Divorced!" she exclaimed when he had finished. "Who says this?"

"A court of English bishops, Your Grace," he told her, "presided over by the new Archbishop of Canterbury, Cranmer."

"No word from Rome?"

"No. And I fear it is too late, Your Grace."

"It is too late for me," Katherine said grimly. "But for my daughter it must not be too late." Mary came forward: a large, brooding, silent girl, with the Tudor roundness of face colored with the somber darkness of her Aragonese blood.

Katherine took her daughter's hand.

"Mary will rule England," she said.

The Spanish ambassador steeled himself for the last shot of ill tidings. "The King," he informed her, "has already married Anne Boleyn."

Although she was prepared for this, the Queen's reaction was that of someone who had been given a blow on the face.

"She has unholy powers!" she cried. "I believe she was sired by the Prince of Darkness to drag down a great king into Hell!"

The ambassador tried to reassure the distracted Queen. "I will go to Rome," he said. "The Emperor will bring the Pope to a decision. Your marriage will be upheld. Any children of this woman, Boleyn, will be illegitimate."

"Is my life in danger?" Katherine wanted to know. She clutched at Mary. "Or hers?"

"I had thought of it," the ambassador admitted grimly. "I have spoken to the King about your safety. I spoke bluntly. Neither he nor the relatives of the woman will dare to harm you."

Her Spanish pride remained with Katherine to uphold her. "There cannot be two queens in the land," she said. "I shall surely maintain my title while I have breath."

He shook his head sadly. "Then I fear some good men will die for your sake," he said. He kissed her hand. "I must leave you."

He left the two women there in the desolate room.

Through the window they could hear the hoofbeats of his galloping horse. The sound soon died away.

Katherine took her daughter's hand and held it tightly.

"You will reign, never fear. God is not mocked!" she said.

Mary did not answer. Her resolute dark face was fixed on the cross that hung against the bare white wall.

Thirty-Three

A crowd was gathering outside the Tower of London. Silent people with shut, blank faces lined the street.

Suddenly bells pealed out, filling the still air with their joyful clangor. At the same moment a pair of men-at-arms came striding down the narrow road, clearing a path through the people and shouting, "Clear! Stand clear!" The crowd reluctantly made way. "Back," the men-at-arms called hoarsely. "Get back!"

Behind them came two sweating workmen, unrolling an enormous carpet of red velvet, covering the filth and refuse of the street with its interwoven symbols, H and A.

Now two files of men-at-arms in royal livery marched out to line the route, standing on either side of it with their backs to the crowd.

It was the day of Anne Boleyn's coronation: Whit-Sunday, the first day of June, 1533.

On Tower Green stood King Henry, most splendidly attired. His head was high, his spirits jaunty, as he held out a sprig of May blossom to Anne.

"There, Nan," he said, smiling like the sun. "For luck."

Brilliant sunshine blazed around the royal pair as the cortege took shape, waiting in readiness for the signal to move to Westminster for the coronation ceremony. First were the heralds in tabards of red and gold. Then came Henry and Anne. Anne seemed almost dwarfed in the stiff coronation robes she wore. Her train was carried by the Mistress of Robes. Then came the courtiers, their plumes waving in the light breeze: Norris, Weston, and Brereton. Behind them Norfolk, Thomas Boleyn, and Cromwell took their places. Other courtiers were strung out behind them. In their midst were George and Elizabeth Boleyn and the new Queen's ladies-in-waiting.

It was a splendid, flawless day, and a brilliant array.

A cannon was fired behind them. The smoke curled up toward the unruffled sky. The cortege began to move.

Out in the street beyond the Tower, all the men-at-arms stood stiffly in place. The eyes of the crowd were all turned toward the Tower. The crowd waited silently.

At last the heralds appeared, the slow-moving procession behind them. The cannon fired off the second shot of the ordained eighteen-gun salute.

Boleyn came into view, leading his wife. Norfolk, walking with George Boleyn, raked the sullen crowd with his eyes.

"How much were they paid to cheer?" Norfolk asked.

"A groat each," Boleyn said. "A thousand of them between here and Westminster."

"They should have got a silver penny each," Norfolk answered wryly. "They'd have thrown their caps in the air for that!"

A woman in the crowd opened her mouth and screamed out: "God save Queen Katherine!"

Cromwell, rigid-faced, muttered, "We've been outbid by the Spanish ambassador!"

Another woman's voice cut through the air.

"Whore!" she screamed shrilly. "King's whore!"

Anne lifted her chin. Henry looked around angrily.

The air crackled as the cannon fired the third shot of the eighteen-gun salute.

And now a man in the crowd took off his hat and waved it over his head. In a high defiant voice he called out, "Long live the Queen!"

"There's an honest fellow," Norfolk remarked.

"Which Queen does he mean, my lord?" retorted Cromwell.

The booing and the shouting swelled.

"Whore!" another voice yelled hoarsely. "Long live the true Queen!"

"Concubine!"

"Long live Queen Katherine!"

Henry and Anne advanced, the smiles frozen on their faces.

"Send the King's slut back to Kent!"

Suddenly Henry bellowed at the heralds: "Play!"

The trumpets were raised to the heralds' lips. The trumpets sounded.

The shouts increased. The sullen crowd had turned angry now, calling out imprecations against Anne. The bells continued to toll, the cannons thundered, the trumpets blared brassily. But it was impossible to drown out the menacing shouts.

Lady Elizabeth called above the din, "They will grow to love her in time!"

Her brother Norfolk called back to her, "Half a crown a head would have done it!"

Cromwell permitted himself a small ironical smile.

"In her case," he said, "a whole crown or nothing."

The cortege inched relentlessly forward to Westminster Abbey.

Thirty-Four

The coronation was over at last, and the royal party had returned to Greenwich.

Anne, now Queen of England, was shown into the room that had been Katherine's. She was still wearing her coronation robes. The crown, borne on a silken cushion, and carried by one of her ladies, had preceded her there. It was her moment of triumph.

She paused for a moment on the threshold. The three ladies-in-waiting who had attended Queen Katherine awaited her, and now they sank to the floor in deep curtsies. Then, without a word, they gathered round Anne and, with the deft assistance of the Mistress of Robes, unfastened her cloak and took it from her shoulders.

King Henry entered the room.

"Out!" he roared. "Out. Your King would have words with his Queen. Out! All of you, out!"

The ladies flew out like startled swallows.

The door swung shut behind them.

Henry turned to Anne.

"Come here," he said. "It's a long time since I kissed a queen." His expression was as joyful as a youth's. He was bursting with the happiness that filled him. No shadow of uncertainty clouded his forehead.

"I have kept every part of my bargain, Nan," he said, glowing. "Shall you be happy now? My Queen, my woman, my—"

" '*Whore*,' the crowd said," she reminded him wryly.

"Damn the Spanish ambassador!" he stormed.

Anne laughed outright. "You must outbid him at the christening, Hal. In four months when I give you a son, I want cheers of joy!"

"Anne," he said tenderly. "Anne, they won't need bribes. It will be the happiest day in the whole history of this kingdom."

With the roar of a young bull he picked her up in his arms and carried her over to the bed.

She filled the room with her shrieks of laughter.

"My lord," she asked, gasping, "would you ravish a woman who is already with child?"

He pulled away from her. "By God, Nan," he said soberly. "Forgive me!"

She flung her arms around his neck and drew him down to her.

"Oh," she cried in a voice full of tenderness, "you great royal fool!"

The sound of pealing bells came pouring through the windows in which the initials "A.B." had already been set, replacing those of Katherine of Aragon.

Thirty-Five

On a day four months later Thomas Boleyn and his wife and son George rode up to Greenwich Palace, where they dismounted and hastened inside.

They sped up to the Queen's quarters.

There was a great commotion in the corridors.

Through the bustle of nurses rushing past them down the hall and into the Queen's room, they could hear Anne's cries.

The Queen was in childbirth.

Cromwell stood at the door with his secretary, waiting.

As Elizabeth hurried into the room, one of the Queen's ladies-in-waiting came hurrying out and collided with her. She looked up, flustered. "Your pardon, Madam," she said, blushing, "but the Queen is—"

Lady Elizabeth recognized the girl. She was a docile, gentle creature, a gentlewoman, Sir John Seymour's daughter. She had been a lady-in-waiting to Queen Katherine; now she served Anne.

"Is it born, Jane?" Elizabeth Boleyn put in. "Is it a boy?"

Jane Seymour stared at her blankly, her eyes wide. "It is nearly time, the midwife says—" Then she fled down the hall.

The Boleyns pushed their way into the chamber where Anne lay, crying out in her labor.

Master Cromwell nodded to his secretary.

"Fetch the King," he said.

Thirty-Six

Henry rode in Richmond Park with the Duke of Norfolk.

"By God," the King cried, "I've waited all my life

for it! All my life as a king I have asked only one thing of Heaven, that it grant me a son to carry on what I leave!"

A horseman came into sight at full gallop. Henry looked up. It was Cromwell's secretary racing toward them.

"Here is my good news, Norfolk!" the King shouted jubilantly.

He put spurs to his horse.

Norfolk stayed behind. He watched Henry and the messenger come together briefly, their horses pawing the air as they were reined in. Then Henry was off at a full gallop and on the air there was the elated sound of his voice coming back to Norfolk.

"A prince!" the King cried.

Norfolk crossed himself with relief.

Now the King's voice came from a distance as he rode away toward the palace. "A prince!" It was like the crowing of a cock at the gates of Heaven, like a battle cry. "A prince!"

Thankfully, Norfolk looked up at the heavens.

There was a rumble of faraway thunder. In the sky, dark rain clouds had begun to gather.

He dug his spurs into his horse's sides and galloped after the King.

Thirty-Seven

Hard pelting rain had begun to beat against the windows of the Queen's chamber.

Anne lay in bed. Her face was pale. Her dark hair,

dank with sweat, streamed across the pillows. The midwife was wrapping her baby in the last of its swaddling clothes and putting it down into an elaborately carved and gilded cradle with the Tudor rose pricked out in gold at its head. Jane Seymour and Madge Shelton, another of the ladies-in-waiting, smoothed the Queen's pillows. At the side of the bed stood the Boleyns: Thomas and Elizabeth and Anne's sister Mary. George hovered nearby. The Queen's doctor moved from the baby to Anne.

"The child is perfectly formed and in good health, Your Grace," he said.

Anne averted her face from the child and burst into a spasm of silent weeping.

"I have failed," she said softly. She pressed her face into the pillows. Her nerve, her self-control, and her certainty had abandoned her for the first time. "I have failed. God help me."

Her father bent over her. It was far too dangerous for them all, he knew, if Anne faltered now.

He glanced up at the ladies-in-waiting.

"Let me be private with her," he told them between clenched teeth.

They backed silently away.

"Don't weep!" he commanded his daughter. "Pinch your cheeks for some color. Sit up and smile, Nan. You are the Queen." He spoke softly and fiercely. "Brazen it out. A girl this time, but a boy the next time. You hear me?"

Anne turned her head.

"She is beautiful?" she asked wanly.

"Yes, she is!" her father told her. "She has beautiful little hands and a beautiful face!"

Anne lifted her head from the pillows.

"Give me the child," she said. "Give me my daughter."

The midwife lifted the infant from the cradle.

"The King's at the door now," George called.

"He must come in, of course," Elizabeth said.

"Not yet—not yet!" Anne said weakly. "Make some excuse. Not quite yet."

"My dear," her mother said in alarm, "it's her father —the King!"

The door had burst open and Henry entered. The doctor and Boleyn greeted him with low bows. The women, with the exception of the midwife, curtsied. Henry ran to see the child in the woman's plump arms. She laid it in the bed beside the Queen.

"Is he well?" Henry demanded. "Is he strong?" He turned to Anne. "Nan, sweet—"

"Yes, Henry?"

"Did I come too soon? Will it tire you to speak?"

"No, Henry. I am glad to see you."

He stared at the child. "I won't say much, nor stay long. I just want to look at you two: the most precious freight a bed ever carried. My queen, and my prince, my son."

"My lord—" Anne began.

"Hush. Rest, my dear, and get strong."

The child suddenly let out a fine healthy bellow.

Henry smiled. "Those are lungs that will out-bellow a Spanish ambassador, eh, Nan? And the eyes—the eyes are clever. I shall call him Edward. It's been a lucky name for English kings, a lucky name and a great name! Heaven has given me more than I asked, for this is a handsome, bold boy's face, and already there's wit behind those eyes!"

He reached out to take the child.

Anne spoke out clearly. "I have borne you a daughter, Your Grace."

Henry stopped. He had not touched the child.

"A daughter?"

"Yes," Anne said.

His face darkened. "Why did no one tell me before I entered this chamber?"

"I wanted to tell you myself, Hal," she answered. She looked down tenderly at the child for a moment. "She has a sweet face. Next time, Hal, it will be a son!"

Thomas Boleyn's thin lips grinned in relief at Anne's courage.

But Henry still stood there, shattered. The thought of a daughter had never once occurred to him. "A

117

daughter!" he echoed. The shock was so great that he could not even feel anger.

"Elizabeth," Anne said. "We shall call her Elizabeth."

Henry pressed his lips together, collecting himself a little.

"Is the child in good health?"

"Perfect, Your Grace," the doctor told him.

"Well, then, it's no fault of anyone. There must be girls as well as boys. If we can have a healthy daughter we can have a healthy son. As you say . . . as you say, Nan." His eyes turned restlessly. He could not wait now to be quit of the room. "So I'll kiss you and leave you, Nan," he blustered. He bent and kissed her quickly. "And God keep all here," he said, hurrying to the door.

"Will you not kiss your daughter, Hal?" Anne called after him.

He paused. "When she's a shade older, my dear. When she's grown a foot or two and is in petticoats, and can run! When she has a brother!"

And he was out the door. He closed it and leaned back against it, breathing heavily.

In the passage outside the Queen's room, Cromwell was waiting.

He stepped forward. He said, bowing, "May I offer Your Grace congratulations?"

Henry peered at him. His nostrils quivered. Then he spat his words into the lawyer's smiling face.

"Get out from under my feet, you whore-son pig!"

Then he strode away.

Thirty-Eight

"Still no word from the King? . . . No answer even to my letter?"

Katherine of Aragon, no longer Henry's wife, no longer England's queen, lay in her bed in the bare country house to which she and her daughter had been banished. Her face was wasted. Her great eyes stared out from hollows, and her bony hands clutched at the coverlet.

Her chaplain, a doctor, and Princess Mary stood by her bedside. The doctor frowned, turned to the chaplain and shrugged.

A waiting woman, old and shabbily dressed, waddled into the room carrying a cup and spoon. She held them out to Katherine.

Wearily, Katherine pushed aside the proffered cup.

"How can he so utterly forget so much?"

"He does not forget, Mother," Mary said bluntly. She was now a girl of sixteen—not beautiful, not even striking, and dressed in the severe old-fashioned style of the Spanish court. But beneath her quiet surface bubbled the wild blood of Henry and the passionate fervor of her mother's people. She had witnessed her mother's unhappiness and had lived through her own companionless, unhappy childhood. What she had seen and suffered had formed a core of terrible inner strength in her. Now, beneath her bewilderment and resentment of her mother's fate and her own destiny, it grew even harder. Her eyes, dry and thoughtful, were fixed on her mother's dying face. "He has no wish to remember, Mother. But rumors from the court say that all is not well with them. There is still no sign of a son. That woman is in despair. They say that already my beloved father's eye has started to wander again."

"Poor Hal," Katherine murmured. "Poor Hal . . ."

"You pity him?" the girl asked, incredulous. What a strange, impossible-to-understand thing this world of grown-up love was!

"Was I not his much-loved wife?" her mother answered. She paused to recover her breath. Then she went on in a thin voice, "And you are his daughter. Unless he has a son born of a true marriage, you are his heir. You must be Queen."

"But now we've another princess," Mary reminded her.

"And you must call her sister. She's of his blood too. Remember that, Mary." For a moment a painful memory swept through her mind. "Oh, Henry!" she cried as though in pain.

Mary studied her mother intently.

"Call her sister!" she said in scorn.

Katherine's hands clutched more tightly at the coverlet. "Remember," she gasped. "When I'm gone—you are first."

She shut her eyes. A moan came from her parched lips.

"Doctor!" Mary cried. "Quickly!"

The doctor and the chaplain bent over the bed.

Suddenly the chaplain fell to his knees beside it and began to pray.

Katherine of Aragon was dead.

"Yes, Mother," Mary promised aloud. "I will be Queen!"

Greater than the grief in Mary's heart was the hard hatred for the woman who had usurped her mother's place, who had caused her to die in banishment, neglected, unhappy, and alone.

Thirty-Nine

They were dancing in the banqueting hall at Green-wich. The musicians had begun the opening bars of a stately sarabande, and now, while Henry and Anne watched from their chairs on the dais, Brereton led Jane Seymour out to perform the figures. Three other ladies-in-waiting followed on the hands of Norris, Weston, and Smeaton. George Boleyn and Norfolk with their ladies also took the floor. Then other courtiers rose to join them in the graceful weaving movements.

Henry's eyes were riveted on Jane.

Anne's eyes were on the King's.

"Touch her," she said, hard-faced, "and I'll have her sent from court!"

The dancers continued to move, smiling gravely, through the intricate pattern of the dance.

Henry stared stonily at them. "Who?" he demanded.

"That half-witted Seymour who is always so tongue-tied and blushing and adoring when you enter my chamber!"

"She's a mere child," he answered lightly.

"But you would get a child by her if you could," she snapped back.

"But not by you, it seems," he answered boorishly, "except for a useless girl. So mind your tongue, or I'll have *you* sent from court to cool your temper, Madam."

Abruptly, Anne rose to her feet and began to make

her way from the hall. The dancing broke off in confusion as the ladies-in-waiting left their partners and hurried away to follow the Queen.

Henry lumbered up from his chair. "Play on," he shouted. "Play on. The Queen is tired, but does not wish to spoil your pleasure. Come, play!" he called to the hesitant musicians. "Jane!" He stepped down and strode across the floor to intercept Jane Seymour. He stood in front of her. "Come, Jane," he said. His voice became soft and coaxing. "I think we shall dance well together. If I lead strongly, will you softly follow?"

A tinge of red suffused the girl's porcelain-white face. Her adoring eyes looked up at him. "I—I hope so, Your Grace," she stammered.

The music began again and the dance started once more, this time with Henry and Jane leading.

Boleyn, sitting on the sidelines with his wife, grasped Lady Elizabeth's arm.

"Again!" she gasped. She bit her lips. "Poor Anne!"

Brereton, Norris, and Weston now stood without their partners, watching. Jane was smiling, and the King's clear laugh rang out.

Her ladies had flocked around Anne, and the group was making its way toward the door.

"Is the wind changing, I wonder?" said Weston.

Norris grinned. "That little ewe won't hold the royal ram beyond the first encounter!"

At the door, Anne stood still for a moment to watch the dancers. Then she raised a finger to summon an officer to her side. She spoke to him in a low voice. He gave her a startled look as he listened to her. "I order you!" she said. Then she swept over, followed by her three ladies.

The music played on. Henry danced on with Jane Seymour.

Master Cromwell, standing unobtrusively beside the door, watched the Queen depart.

Forty

The Queen was preparing for bed. A lady-in-waiting was helping her into a gown while another put away her dress and jewels. Her long hair cascaded over her shoulders and down her back.

There was a hammering on the door.

The ladies-in-waiting glanced in alarm at the Queen. She turned to the nearest. "Let them in," she said.

The frightened girl crept forward and cautiously opened the door. Two men-at-arms holding torches stood in the passageway. Henry brushed past them and strode into the chamber with Cromwell a pace or two behind him.

The lady-in-waiting hesitated.

"Leave us," Anne told her.

Silently, the ladies departed.

Anne faced the King defiantly.

"Where is Jane Seymour?" he demanded. "Cromwell tells me that when the dance ended she was taken away under guard."

"In Northumberland," she answered wildly. "And a very good place for her."

"Her brothers have made it plain that they resent the slur you cast on her in sending her from court."

"I don't care for her. She has the face of a sheep, and a sheep's simpering manners. But not the morals. I don't want her near me."

"You will bring her back."

"I think not. No. If you want her near you, why, find a place for her in your palace at Whitehall. While I am here, Jane Seymour must lie elsewhere."

Henry turned to the lawyer. "Speak to her, Cromwell."

Cromwell said quietly, "The truth is, Your Grace, that you are on slippery ground. The people cry down your name more and more. There used to be a penalty for speaking against you. There's none now. And the people take advantage of it. They say you are the 'Witch Queen.' "

Anne's eyes dilated. "Are we ruled, then, by superstition?"

"It happens, Your Grace, that you stand for something the people don't want. The old queen still lives in the heart of the people. They say that her daughter is the heir, and yours the bastard."

"Am I at the mercy of the people?"

"We're all at the mercy of the people," he replied. "They hate you, Madam, for displacing Queen Katherine and tearing the King from the church, as they hate me for despoiling the monasteries. But the King they truly love. You and I, Madam, live in the protection of the King."

"So?"

"So—in Parliament, which speaks for the people, there is a bill. It is called the Act of Succession. It makes your daughter the King's heir, and Katherine's daughter, Mary, illegitimate. If the King does not wish it, the Act of Succession will not be passed."

"And so, my dear," put in Henry, "be a little less absolute in what you'll have and what you'll not have!"

"Would you sacrifice the child of our love to get a silly little harlot brought back to court?" she flashed back at him.

He shrugged. "One daughter is much as another. I am indifferent as to which is named bastard when I am dead."

"And if I bring Jane Seymour back, will you have Parliament pass this Act of Succession?"

"Yes."

Anne burst out into sudden laughter.

"What a liar you are! What good is that Act unless every man in the kingdom who has power to accept my child as the legitimate heir first swears an oath of fealty to you as head of the church. And if they do not, Act of Succession or no Act of Succession, they will cry out that my child is the bastard, and there's an end."

"Go," Henry told Cromwell curtly.

The door closed discreetly behind the lawyer.

"If you love me, don't defy me," Henry said. "Bring her back."

"I love you now," she told him in a low voice. "I shall go to my grave loving you, no doubt, and hating you."

"Then bring her back!"

"I will bring her back to my court," she went on in measured tones, "if the oath is sworn by all men of power, high and low. But those who refuse must die."

"It was you who once said they must not die."

"And it was you who once said they must, and now so say I!"

"Let me off from this, Nan. I can't kill these men."

"You've killed before!"

"One learns a little. Never since Buckingham have I touched a man in high place, one I respected, one whose death might become a symbol. Nan," he implored, "if you love me, forget the succession."

She answered steadily, "But if you remember how it all came about, and how your word is dishonored, how can you look in my eyes and say our daughter will not succeed?"

"Because I cannot look on these deaths in all honesty! Other deaths, but not these! Look at me, Nan. Is it fitting I should be head of a church—King and Pope in one—a monumental, tragic farce for which so many must die? Could you sign these death warrants?"

"Oh, King of England!" she cried out. "You blind King! I'd sign tèn thousand to die rather than warm that white-faced serpent you love and disinherit my blood! Let the blood run and the fires burn! It's that, or else it's my blood and Cromwell's and Elizabeth's. Cromwell knows that, your butcher-cleaver man knows that! Send him out to implement these deaths and let it be done quickly. Let there be no mistaking, no leniency, no mercy! High or low they will sign—or depart without entrails. And you will keep your word to me, unloved though I may be." Her voice broke. "I wish that I were loved, but I am not, and so I shall be Queen of this island, and Elizabeth shall be Queen!"

There was a pause.

"No," he said at last. "But you're beautiful when you're angry." He stepped toward her. "Now, if we had a son . . . Help me to prove that I can father kings!"

She held out her hand to fend him off. "What do you mean?"

"For Elizabeth, no. For her I will not commit these murders. But if we had a male heir—" He pressed toward her. "Your son and mine—"

Her hand still held him at arm's length. "I can be angrier than you've seen me yet, and not beautiful! I know where your heart is. It's not with me."

"What has the heart to do with the getting of kings?" he demanded. "I am not young. I am not true. I'm bitter and expert and aging and venomous—not to be trusted. It's your misfortune that you love me now that I no longer love you. Yet at this moment I want you: because of the anger and the flash of blood in your face—" His voice was urgent, his eyes eager.

"No," she said.

"And Nan," he pleaded, "if you give me a prince, things may change. Even I may change!"

"No," she said again. "Not unless you kill them: More and Houghton and Fisher, and all who will not sign. Not unless Elizabeth is your heir."

Her face was unrelenting. Her arms still held him away from her.

He squared his shoulders. "I will put them to death, then," he said. "See now: I rob and murder at your order. And I commit sacrilege as well."

"You do what you wish to do," she flung back fiercely, "and call it my deed." He put his ardent arms around her. "I hate you. I hate your desire," she said, "and mine." She pulled away from him.

"Things could change," he pleaded. "Even I. I loved you once. I saw that fire in your face!" He pressed his burning mouth against hers. "Give me a son!"

Her resistance slowly subsided. And now the kiss she returned to him was as fierce and impatient as his own.

Forty-One

Sir Thomas More was leaving the Tower of London. He had been confined there, at the King's will, for many months. He had refused to sign the oath.

At his trial, the King's one-time chancellor had offered a brilliant defense, but the King's trust in him was changed to vengeful dislike; and the judges, pressed by the royal will, had pronounced him guilty of treason.

A scaffold had been raised on the Tower Green, and a crowd as sullen and silent as that which had lined the streets to curse Anne on the day of her coronation stood and watched as Sir Thomas was led out of the tower between a file of soldiers. He looked haggard and ill: his body was already broken. Little more than his spirit remained to sustain him on this final walk.

Sir William Kingston, portly and dignified, the Constable of the Tower, was waiting for him at the foot of the ladder to the scaffold.

More glanced at the ladder, and a touch of his old humor returned. "I pray you, Master Kingston, see me safe up," he begged. "As for my coming down, let me shift for myself."

Kingston took his arm and assisted him up. The black-masked headsman reached down to help him onto the platform.

For a second Sir Thomas looked into the unblinking eyes of his executioner. Then he turned to address the crowd.

"Good people—" he began.

Kingston raised his hand and signaled to the soldiers. They immediately struck a continuous, heavy roll of drums to drown More's voice.

More turned to the Constable of the Tower with a questioning glance.

"The King's orders," Kingston said, apology and deference in his uneasy voice. "You must not be heard."

"Then I will not speak," More replied simply.

Kingston waved the drums into silence.

"I die the King's good servant," Sir Thomas More said quietly, "but God's first."

He knelt at the block. The drums rolled again. The executioner was ready.

The ax flashed down.

So died the most sensitive and far-seeing man of his time. In one stroke, the man of letters and of action, chancellor and Christian humanist, statesman and reformer—the man who epitomized all that was best in the medieval world—became the tragic hero of his century.

He had won from Henry a martyr's palm.

Forty-Two

For the second time the Queen lay screaming in childbirth.

In the lamplight around her bed stood the doctor, the midwife, and the Queen's parents, waiting for Anne to be delivered. They watched anxiously. Things were not going well. Anne's face, drained of blood, thrashed about on the pillows.

At last, and with great pain, it came: a stillborn boy.

Anne's eyes were dilated like those of a madwoman. But her father did not wait to console her this time. He hurried to the door, past the hushed ladies-in-waiting.

Norfolk waited for him in the passage outside the Queen's room.

Norfolk reached for Boleyn's sleeve. "Well?"

"A son," Boleyn said dully. "Born dead."

Norfolk's lips twisted grimly. "She has miscarried of her saviour."

Boleyn did not reply. He knew too well the truth of Norfolk's words.

Forty-Three

It was Cromwell, quiet and ubiquitous, who came to Henry as the King lay in his bed.

"I have ill news, Your Grace."

"What news?"

"The Queen is brought to bed of a son, and it is born dead."

Henry repeated, not yet comprehending, "A son. Born dead."

Cromwell nodded.

Henry squinted at him. "I don't trust you in this."

"I didn't trust anyone else, Your Grace. I went to see it. And it's a son, and dead."

The King sank back against the pillows.

"A son," he mused. "Born dead, like the sons of Katherine. Born, and a son; but cursed with the curse of God because I've had her sister, or because—well, for whatever reason, it was dead. Oh, my God, help me! What do You want of me? Was this girl not to Your mind? Not ever? Or am I not to Your mind?" He stared dementedly at Cromwell. "But I am the King," he raged, "God's chosen, potent and virile. I am a man. The woman's failed me." His eyes narrowed in his tormented face. "Yes—that's it! She's failed me. I must look elsewhere."

Shadowed by the heavy bed-hangings, Master Cromwell listened.

Forty-Four

In the morning, Cromwell was once more listening to the King.

"I am accursed!" Henry shouted. His face was rumpled and unshaven. His robe hung open. It was clear to his minister that the King had been through a night of sleepless Hell.

"A live daughter and a dead son," Henry bellowed. "Did I accept excommunication for this? Did I send More and Fisher and Houghton to their deaths for this?" His fingers raked distractedly through his uncombed beard. "She cannot bear me a living son! And this on the day they buried Katherine. Ah, God, the irony!" His narrowed eyes bored into Cromwell's. "Very well, then, if Anne cannot give me a male heir, I shall rid myself of her," he decided.

"Sire," Cromwell told him cautiously, "with Katherine's death, Anne is too firmly the Queen."

"Find a way!" Henry blustered. "Find a legal way. I will divorce Anne. Divorce is like killing. After the first time it doesn't seem so difficult."

"Your Grace," protested Cromwell, "we asserted English law before. Anne is now Queen by law."

Henry impatiently waved the lawyer's argument aside.

"All right, all right. I got the divorce from Katherine in good faith, but since then I've realized an impediment to my marriage to Anne. I had a child by Anne's sister, Mary. That, too, was incestuous."

Cromwell said in a dry tone, "We used the incest excuse last time. We can't make a habit of it."

Henry gave him a shrewd glance. "Anne has no Pope or Spanish Emperor to uphold her, and the people hate her."

"She'd fight," Cromwell insisted. "Her sister was married when she bore your child. You couldn't prove that it was not her husband's."

"For God's sake, Cromwell," the King burst out in exasperation, "whose side are you on?"

"The King's, Sire," he replied smoothly. "Your Grace can't afford to start all that again."

Henry suddenly reached out, seized him, and shook him.

"Do you know of another way? You tied me to her —you! You! Now you find a way to be rid of her!" He suddenly let go of Cromwell and pushed him aside with a powerful sweep of his arm that nearly sent him reeling.

Cromwell recovered his balance. There was a pause while Cromwell stood reflecting, with Henry regarding him with such close attention that it seemed as though Henry were trying to read Cromwell's thoughts through his forehead.

"Perhaps," the lawyer suggested hesitatingly after a few moments, "perhaps in her own life . . . ?"

"Ha! *Her* life . . . the contract to marry Percy! He had her." He clapped Cromwell on the shoulder. "That's it, you crawling toad!"

"No, Your Grace, not her past life." He lowered his eyes, casting his glance down at the floor. "The present," he said. He paused. "The rumors that she has a lover."

"What?" Henry roared. "My wife? I, a cuckold? You're mad!"

"If I could prove it?"

"Invent it, you mean, with falsified evidence."

"Adultery is high treason," Cromwell reminded him gently. "The penalty is death, Your Grace."

"Anne?" Henry spluttered. "Get out! Get out!"

132

Cromwell made a humble bow and started to leave. As he was opening the door the King's voice came roaring at him.

"Cromwell!"

Cromwell turned.

Then he closed the door again and went back to the King.

Forty-Five

Mark Smeaton was a little bewildered to have received such an invitation. He was also pleased that Thomas Cromwell, the King's right hand, had singled him out and sent a request that Smeaton dine with him that night. And so, in peacock bright attire and in excellent humor, Smeaton appeared at the appointed hour.

He was, if anything, even more bewildered when no other members of the royal household joined them.

Cromwell, dressed in rich but sober clothes, greeted Smeaton in a flatteringly cordial fashion; and it was not long before his host ushered him into the dining chamber where two brawny retainers waited to serve them.

"I am honored, Master Cromwell," Smeaton observed agreeably. "As a rule, when I am invited to supper I am expected to sing for it."

"As you do for the Queen?" Cromwell remarked with a faint smirk.

The singer laughed openly. "That, for me, is pleasure, my lord. She wishes me to be the first music teacher to the Princess."

"Please sit," Cromwell said with brisk courtesy. "There are no other guests."

The servants poured wine for them, and then proceeded to bring platters of food.

"I did not know, Master Cromwell, that music interested you in any special way," Smeaton remarked.

"It doesn't," Cromwell replied. "I am interested in the Queen. And you know her so well."

Smeaton turned in surprise. Then caution tugged at him. He suddenly recalled that, after all, no one in the King's service really trusted the upstart attorney. He said with a shrug, "I am merely a servant."

Now it was Cromwell's turn to lean forward. "I have the King's express orders," he confided, "to protect the Queen's person. We have learned of threats. Many hate her. I am dining you, Smeaton, as I will dine others, to get to know those whom I may trust."

"I see, I see," Smeaton replied guardedly.

"And it is true that she likes to have you close to her, is it not?"

Smeaton smiled expansively, responding to Cromwell's frankness and trust.

"Without boasting," he said, "I believe that she prefers me to many. She prefers my style to the Italian. It is nearer to the manner she learned to love in the French court."

Cromwell stretched out his hand to refill the singer's wine cup. His face was bland. "She learned to love like a Frenchwoman?"

Smeaton was still happily unaware of the direction in which the interview led, or of the insinuation in Cromwell's manner. "Yes," he responded, "simple tunes sung with—" Then he suddenly understood the lawyer's drift. He threw his head back and laughed.

Cromwell was no longer smiling.

"You would be wiser not to laugh. It is a more valuable asset than a pleasant singing voice."

Smeaton said with a smile, "*I* make my way by singing. I've no desire to go any further by any other route."

"Come now," Cromwell coaxed. "There are only two reasons for you to be constantly in the Queen's apartments. You love her, or—" the coaxing tone became, abruptly, one of ice—"you are in the pay of Spain."

"I—I go when I'm sent for," Smeaton answered nervously.

"To love, or spy? Which?"

Smeaton started to rise, but the meaty hands of the two retainers kept him clamped in his chair.

"Which?" Cromwell insisted. Then he permitted himself to smile. "You are too simple to spy. I know that. So it is love. You love her."

One of the retainers slipped a noosed rope over Smeaton's shoulders and drew the cord tight, pinning the singer to the chair.

"No," Smeaton cried. "No!"

The smile remained fixed on Cromwell's face.

"You do not love your Queen?"

"Well—yes, it is true—I do love her, as my Queen." Smeaton was too terrified to stir. His eyes were fixed on Cromwell's.

"And she loves you?" his interrogator continued.

"No, sir. Of course not," he protested.

"Barton," Cromwell called. "Come out here. Bring your papers."

Cromwell's secretary emerged from behind a screen. In his hands were a goose quill, an inkpot, and a sheaf of papers.

"Read the last line but one," Cromwell commanded.

In a voice without expression, the secretary read out: "Well, yes, it is true, I do love her."

Cromwell gestured to him to sit at the end of the table and continue writing notes.

"What are you trying to make me say?" gasped Smeaton.

"The truth: that you are the Queen's lover."

Smeaton began to struggle frantically against the rope. "No!" he cried. "No!"

"You first lay with her in February," the lawyer said.

"Never! I never—"

135

One of the retainers placed a tourniquet around Smeaton's head. The cord cut into his forehead.

"On the eighteenth of February," Cromwell resumed.

"No!"

Cromwell nodded at the servant, who began to twist the stick in the tourniquet.

The accuser's voice was lightly mocking. "Surely you remember such an important date?"

"No!"

The veins on Smeaton's temples stood out. His handsome features were contorted.

The servant gave the stick another twist.

"Come," Cromwell wheedled. "Try to remember."

Smeaton was sweating in pain and terror. "No," he cried. "No!"

The stick twisted once again.

Smeaton became hideous in his agony. The pain was unbearable. A scream broke out of him.

"Yes!"

Forty-Six

Cromwell brought the singer's confession to Henry early the next morning.

The King's eyes raced over the document. Then, thrusting it aside, he demanded, "It is true, Cromwell?"

"The truth is what the judges will find, what the King will decide."

"Don't juggle words with me!" Henry said hotly. "Did it happen?"

"As you see, Your Grace," came Cromwell's smooth reply, "Smeaton confesses."

"Under torture?"

"Scarcely less than is customary. He implicates the others: Brereton, Norris, Weston. They are all close to you, all with easy access to the Queen."

After the first words Henry was no longer listening.

"God knows she could," he reflected aloud. "And I've given her cause. But you, Cromwell, you have reasons for wishing her guilty. You need a scapegoat to blame for the robbery of the monasteries and the church."

"Sire—" began Cromwell.

"And I need a scapegoat," the King went on. "I, too, need to find her guilty. And you know that. You play on that."

"Sire, if you wish to accuse me—"

"I accuse both of us! I want to marry elsewhere, and if Anne were dead I'd be free. And you saw this, and so you put the temptation before you, you liar, you butcher, you piece of filth from the London streets!" He paused. "And yet," he said, shaking his head, "she may truly be guilty!"

"So Mark Smeaton says," Cromwell assured him. "And then there is also the matter of her brother which I was able to discover."

Henry's eyes were hot, his mouth dry. "Yes, that above all!" Again he paused. When he spoke at last his voice had turned to steel. "Let her be tried. Let her be tried by a group of peers. Let her uncle, Norfolk, preside. Let her have justice in the eyes of the world. Arrest her. Arrest them all!"

He signed the warrants that Cromwell had set out on the table before him.

"Yes, Your Grace," Cromwell said deferentially. He took up the signed papers and started to leave the King's chamber.

Henry's voice halted him.

"And, Cromwell, if she speaks in her defense, I wish

to be where I may hear her speak. But I do not wish to be seen."

"Yes, Your Grace."

He went.

Henry Tudor looked thoughtfully after him. His fingers beat on the table in a heavy tattoo, like the drum at an execution.

Forty-Seven

The Queen played with her daughter, alone in her chambers.

It had amused the Queen to attach a court train to the child's shoulders.

"Anyone can walk, Elizabeth," she said. "But can you walk with a train?"

She stepped back and beckoned to the tiny princess.

"Now," she called. "Come on. Hold up your head." Elizabeth began to toddle gravely toward her. "No, don't look round. It'll follow you like a kitten's tail. There!" Elizabeth had reached the safety of her mother's outstretched arms. Anne pressed the child to her. "Oh," she sang out, "what a queen it will make some day!"

There was an urgent knock on the door.

"Enter," Anne called.

Madge Shelton fluttered into the room. Two men-at-arms stood at attention in the doorway behind her, framing the tall figure of the Duke of Norfolk.

"Madam," Madge cried, "the Duke of Norfolk insists—"

Anne stood up. "Uncle! This is a rare honor, nowadays! But why were you not announced?"

"Get out!" Norfolk growled at Madge Shelton.

With a frightened look at her mistress, the girl sped from the room.

Norfolk turned to Anne. "Brace yourself, girl. I have a warrant for your arrest."

"For my arrest?" She let out a little laugh. "That's a poor joke, uncle."

"It is no joke, niece. I could have let others bring it, but I thought I could do it more gently than some."

"What—" Her voice faltered for a moment. "What am I to be arrested for?"

He remained silent.

"But why? What for?" she insisted. "I am the Queen."

Norfolk's face flushed with embarrassment. "For—" He held out the paper with a jerky motion. "It says here for adultery."

"But—this is—"

"Niece, it's pure nonsense, but here it is. You will take a few things and come."

"Adultery? With whom?"

"Smeaton, Norris," he answered gruffly. "And others."

Anne laughed. "For a moment I thought you were serious."

"I am. I'm to take you to the Tower. There's to be a trial. I am to preside."

Anne realized now that Norfolk was truly in earnest, but the accusation against her was so fantastic that she was torn between terror and wild laughter.

"But I'm—my child, she's the King's heir—surely—"

Norfolk broke in, "You're to leave her with your women."

"My women—then what women may I take with me?"

"You must come at once, Anne. You'll be furnished with attendants at the Tower."

The grimness of Norfolk's face quelled the Queen's lingering laughter. Now fear seized her completely.

"Elizabeth!" she cried.

She rushed to hold the child tightly in her arms.

"Elizabeth!"

Then Norfolk gently drew her away and the child was left alone.

Forty-Eight

Anne was taken by boat that night to the Tower of London.

It tied up at the Traitor's Gate.

Sir William Kingston and a small escorting party waited on the landing dock to receive her. Behind them stood the yeomen of the guard.

Anne was helped out of the boat by her uncle Norfolk. She looked up. Behind the reception committee, the flickering light of black-smoking torches picked up the dampness of the stone walls.

The Queen repressed a shudder. "Master Kingston," she asked apprehensively, "shall I be shut in a dungeon?"

"No, Madam," he told her gently. "You will be lodged near the room where you lay on the night before your coronation."

The tears, long held back, came at last. She raised her hands to her pale face to hide them. "Jesus have mercy on me!"

Norfolk took her firmly by the arm. Gently he guided her as they moved off, up the slimy steps.

The solemn escort followed.

The stone pavement resounded under their footsteps as Anne was led to the tower room which was to be hers. Anne and her escort made their way through a tiny passage: the room itself, bare and cheerless, opened up at the end of it. Kingston and Norfolk followed her in.

A gray-haired woman in a dark gown dropped into a curtsy before the Queen.

"I am Lady Kingston, Madam, and will wait upon you, whatever your wishes are."

"Will you?" Anne said. "Then go away. Leave me."

Lady Kingston looked up at her husband for guidance.

"I fear, Madam, that she must stay," Kingston answered gravely. "Every word spoken to you or by you must be reported."

"Send them away, Norfolk," Anne pleaded.

He turned and waved them out of the room.

She paced the floor restlessly. The walls caged her in. She flung out her arms as though to keep them from pressing too closely upon her. "Shall I ever be allowed to walk out and look at the sky? Shall I ever be free?"

She moved to the window and looked down.

Through its small panes she could see the Tower Green, where guards stood holding up torches. Through the curls of dark smoke she could make out a strange scene. Five men were being brought into the tower under guard. They were in chains. Their fine clothes were ripped and bore the signs of struggle. Then the torchlight suddenly flared up and in their bright flash she could make out the men's faces: Smeaton, Norris, Brereton, Weston and— But she could not see clearly who the fifth man was.

Norfolk was at her side when she turned. Terror encompassed her again.

"Norris—Weston—His friends! His friends since the day I first met him! And they are accused with me?"

"Yes," Norfolk said.

"And he is willing to kill them to get rid of me? To kill his closest companions?"

Norfolk nodded.

Anne looked through the window again. She could see the fifth figure now. He was manacled. He moved, and his face turned upward toward the windows.

It was George Boleyn.

"George!" she cried. "Why have they arrested him?"

Norfolk stepped back into the shadows so that she could not see his embarrassed face. "He is also accused of being your lover."

"Incest!" She was stunned. A long moment passed before she spoke again. When she did, her voice was very quiet. "God help me, the King is mad. I am doomed. I see it now. While I live and remain Queen, Elizabeth remains heir. Dead, I make sheep-faced Jane Seymour most undoubted Queen and any son of hers by Henry most undoubted heir, ahead of my Elizabeth. So, to suit Henry's plans, I must die. You must try me, uncle. And Cromwell will see that I am declared guilty, innocent as I am. I see it clearly now. I must die."

Forty-Nine

The trial began, taking place in a hall in the Tower. Norfolk served as judge; Cromwell as prosecutor. A group of peers listened to the evidence and pretended, at least, to sift it.

Henry Norris, Francis Weston, Mark Smeaton, and

William Brereton were tried first. All through the proceedings Anne remained seated in the court, listening as the defendant. Henry, too, was present, hidden from the sight of all in an alcove screened by a tapestry drawn across the opening.

The time came at last for Anne herself to face the court.

Cromwell, as prosecutor, addressed her.

"Your Grace," he began coldly, "you are accused of high treason in that you, being the lawfully wedded wife of our sovereign lord the King, did commit adultery. I ask that you answer my questions."

Anne held her head high. "By what lawful authority am I called here?" she demanded with a flash of the pride that had captivated the pursuing King. "I am your Queen and, as such, share the King's immunity from arrest and trial."

"If you will recall, Your Grace," Cromwell went on blandly, "your friends Norris, Weston, Smeaton and Brereton were tried, found guilty, and condemned ten days ago. If they are guilty, then you are guilty."

"Did they plead guilty?"

"They were found guilty!"

"They were innocent," she declared, "as I am innocent. Any man, no matter who he is, who says the contrary is a liar."

Behind the arras, Henry's eyes flashed anger, although he squirmed, at the same time, with guilt.

Cromwell bowed slightly to Norfolk in the judge's seat. "My Lord," he said, "the warrant of treason was issued by the direction of the King. That is sufficient to give this tribunal jurisdiction." He gave a small dry cough. "However, so that there may be no possibility of doubt as to the guilt of the Queen, will my Lord call the first witness?"

"Call the Earl of Rochford," Norfolk instructed the Court.

"George Boleyn, Earl of Rochford, come into Court!" the usher called out.

The yeomen of the guard brought Boleyn forward. He stood near Anne, facing their uncle Norfolk. A look of contempt masked his face.

Anne felt her heart break at the sight of him. How aged he looked, how ravaged!

"Read the indictment," Norfolk commanded.

In a high, expressionless voice, the usher of the Court read it out: "George Boleyn, you are accused of high treason in that on certain days and dates hereinafter specified you did commit adultery with Anne, Queen of England, being your own sister in the flesh, an act of incest."

"No!" Anne cried out. "It is not true!"

Cromwell cut her off. "It is not your turn to speak," he said severely. He turned to George Boleyn. "How do you plead, guilty or not guilty?"

"You are a foul liar." George Boleyn pronounced the words with utter disdain. "And my judges are your creatures."

Cromwell's features remained impassive. "Stand up, Thomas Boleyn, Earl of Wiltshire!"

Thomas Boleyn slowly rose to his feet. He looked neither at Anne nor at George but stared blindly ahead of him.

"Do you recognize these two accused here present known as Anne and George Boleyn as issue of your body?"

"I do," he responded.

"Look at them, my lord!"

Although Boleyn knew that he was in danger of losing all unless he kept the favor of the King, yet he could not bring himself to do more than flick an eye in the direction of his children.

"By the same mother, Elizabeth Howard, daughter of the Duke of Norfolk—" Cromwell went on.

Boleyn's brother-in-law shifted uneasily in the judge's seat.

"—And therefore," Cromwell intoned relentlessly, "full brother and sister in the flesh, so that their lying together would be incest?"

"Yes." The Court had to strain to hear Boleyn's reply.

"For which the penalty is death," Cromwell pursued. "Proper evidence on this matter will be introduced later. Remove the prisoner."

He smiled a little, returning George Boleyn's contempt.

Thomas Boleyn's anguish showed so plainly that Norfolk cut in rapidly, "That is all, my lord. As father of the accused you are now excused from the duty as judge and may leave."

George Boleyn was already being marched out through the prisoners' door. His father left the Court through another.

"Call Mark Smeaton," Cromwell demanded.

"Mark Smeaton, come into Court," the usher's deep voice rang out into the hush that surrounded them.

And now Mark Smeaton was led in, in chains. His clothes were tattered and filthy. His good looks were gone, his will broken. A savage weal cut across his forehead: the mark of the rope.

Cromwell stood back in order to address his words to the whole court of peers. "My Lords, this man was tried as a commoner; he confessed and was found guilty of adultery with the Queen by a jury of his own order. He will give evidence against the Queen."

"Interrogate him," Norfolk said.

The King's prosecutor threw back his narrow shoulders with a gesture that revealed his entire confidence.

"Smeaton, did you have carnal relations with the Queen?" he asked.

Smeaton had been staring at the floor. Now he raised his head and looked at Anne. Tears were streaming down his cheeks. Anne's look of cold disdain suddenly melted and turned to compassion.

"Smeaton," Cromwell repeated sternly, "did you lie with the Queen?"

"No!" Smeaton suddenly shouted back at him.

In his curtained alcove, the King rose abruptly from his chair and then sank back again.

The hall was filled with a hum of surprise.

Cromwell was taken aback. For a brief moment he lost his customary detachment. Then his confidence swept back. "There is mercy only for those that tell the truth. Four men have been found guilty on your evidence. Was that evidence perjury? You confessed to your own guilt knowing the penalty for treason; knowing, unless the King is merciful, that you will be hanged, cut down while you still live and disemboweled, and your heart torn out of your body while it still beats." Smeaton closed his eyes and groaned. "The King will not be merciful if you lie," the relentless lawyer went on. "Did you have carnal relations with the Queen?"

Smeaton bit his lips. Then terror overcame the little courage he had left. "Yes!" he cried, trembling. "Yes!"

Anne turned to the judge. "My lord of Norfolk, may I question this man?"

"I have not finished!" Cromwell shot out.

Norfolk leaned forward. "Justice must be seen to be done, Master Cromwell." He turned to Anne. "Proceed, Your Grace."

"Thank you, my lord." Anne stepped slowly forward until she was facing Smeaton. "Mark," she said quietly, "look at me."

He hung his head and looked away.

"I know well that you have been tortured. But tell them the truth, Mark," she urged. "Have courage!"

"It is true," Smeaton murmured.

"Write that!" Cromwell flashed his hand at the clerk who sat with an inkhorn beside him, writing in a large book. "He says the charge is true!"

"They have promised you your life, haven't they, Mark," the Queen whispered, "if you lie for them? They will break the promise. It would not be safe to leave you alive."

Smeaton's lips moved, muttering inaudible words.

"He says the charge is true, for the third time," Cromwell crowed. "Write it down! We have our evidence."

Anne touched Smeaton's bruised cheek with her fingers. "Poor gentle singer," she said. "Isn't it better, if you are to die, that you die with the truth upon your lips?"

Desperately, Smeaton moved his cheek away from Anne's touch. "I am guilty," he gasped out. "I was guilty with the Queen. Let me go now. She came to my bed. Let me go! She came to my bed! I swear it!"

Cromwell's eyes flashed. "Even when she tells him

he will die anyway, he still admits his guilt! Write that.
Take him out!"

The yeomen stepped forward, yanking Smeaton by
the arms, and started to march him away.

A hitherto unheard voice now rang through the hall.
"No! Wait!"

The King had thrust aside the arras and appeared
from the alcove.

The hall was filled with consternation. The members
of the Court rose and bowed. Henry, however, paid no
attention to them and they gradually subsided into
their chairs.

Anne, too, bowed. "Ah!" she cried, half-mocking.
"My husband—the King!"

For a moment Henry looked into her face. Then he
strode over to where Smeaton stood between the yeomen.

"When did the Queen come to your bed? How
many times?"

Smeaton's head hung down. "Many times . . ."

Henry grasped him by the hair and lifted his head.
"When?"

"I don't remember."

The King released his hold and stepped back.

"You will remember. Call it to mind, Smeaton, or
you'll speak with those who can jog your memory.
Where did you couch with the Queen, my wife?"

"York Place," Smeaton gasped.

"You lie. It could never have happened at York
Place. You slept in a room with two others."

"No," cried Smeaton desperately. "No, it was at
Windsor."

Henry's mouth curled in scorn. "Fool! She went to
Windsor only with me. Can you find no better lie?"

"It was many places," the singer babbled wildly.
"She came to my bed. It was wherever you like, when-
ever you like. Oh, God help me! Let me go free. I'll
say whatever you like!"

"Did Cromwell promise you your life if you said
this?"

"My lord!" Cromwell cried.

Henry knocked the pen and book from the clerk's

147

hand. "Cease this pen-scratching! Answer me, Smeaton! Did he say you would live?"

"Yes," Smeaton replied.

"He lied to you, Smeaton. You're to die, musician. Say what you like, you're to die! Speak now without lying, for it gains you nothing."

"Why am I to die?" Smeaton implored piteously.

"You're to die in any case, whatever's said from here on. And now that you know that, what happened between you and the Queen?"

Smeaton closed his eyes for a moment. Then he seemed to come to himself. He looked full at Anne. "Between the Queen and me?" he said. "Nothing. She was kind and pleasant and just. I would not hurt her. But they've broken me with ropes and irons and wooden wedges. I—"

"Take him out," Henry ordered.

As the men dragged the musician out, Henry turned his steady regard on Anne. She returned his look with a tantalizing smile.

"And yet—" he said. "And yet it could be true!"

Without another word, he turned on his heel and strode out of the Court.

Fifty

Anne Boleyn's doom was sealed. She knew it with every hammerstroke that came from outside her window in the Tower. Out there on the green the workmen were building the scaffold for her execution.

It was the eighteenth day of the month of May, 1536.

Anne turned from the window, trying to shut out of her ears the incessant sound of the nails being hammered into her scaffold. She sat down at a small desk. On the desk lay a paper covered in marks, and with the years dividing the marks at intervals. She stared blankly at it. And then, to comfort herself, she spoke aloud.

"If I were to die now—but I must not die yet, not yet. It's been too brief: a few weeks and days. How many days, I wonder, since I gave myself, to that last day when he—when he left me and I saw him no more?

"For six years: this year, and this and this and this," she struck through the years, one at a time, "I did not love him." She stopped and looked away from the paper, reflecting. "And then I did. Then I was his. I can count the days I was his in hundreds." Once more she began to tick off the marks. "The days we bedded" (tick), "married" (tick), "bore Elizabeth" (tick), "cooled" (tick), "hated" (tick), "lusted" (tick), "bore a dead child" (tick), "which condemned me" (tick), "to death" (tick). In all, one thousand days. It comes to just a thousand days out of the years. Strangely, just a thousand; and of that thousand, one when we were both in love. Only one when our loves met and overlapped and were both mine and his! When I no longer hated him, he began to hate me, except for that one day. And the son we had, the one son, born of our hate and lust, died in my womb . . ."

There was the sound of keys rattling in the cell door. She did not look round. "I'm not hungry," she called out. "Take the food and leave me," and she went on with her brooding count.

"Nan," a voice said behind her. "Was it true?"

She turned and rose, suddenly pale.

Henry stood there in the cell.

"Was it true?" he said again. His voice was anguished. "You were no virgin when I met you first. You told me as much. You knew what it was to have men."

149

She said slowly, "Have you fallen into your own trap, my Lord? Any evidence you have against me you yourself bought and paid for. Do you now begin to believe it?"

"Nan," he pleaded. "The Court still sits to decide your verdict. I cannot wait for a court to decide upon your guilt. I have to know for myself, to hear if from your lips."

"Whether I was unfaithful to you?"

"Yes! Just that! Whether you were unfaithful to me while I loved you! But I'll never know. Whether you say aye or no, I won't be sure either way, fool that I am, that all men are!"

"There are fools and fools, King Henry," she answered. "You've shut me up here to be tried for adultery and treason toward you. I'm tried, and those with me, as if in a coffin, with the lid closed, no evidence, no voice, no air to breathe, no cellmates for us but torture, or lies, or false promises. You've done this because you love elsewhere and you want to forget me, to go on, to have sons." Her eyes were bitter. "And with me it's easy. It's only a death, not like that years-long tug of worlds you had to go through with Katherine. So you do this, and I know it. But now you come here to make sure whether there was truly adultery, because that would touch your manhood, or your pride. And you crouch and listen, a cat in a corner, watching the pet mouse before it dies. And then you come out, to make sure! And even so, my heart and my eyes are glad of you. Fool of all women that I am, I'd glad of you here!" She turned her face away. "Go, then. Keep your pride of manhood. You know about me now."

"Nan—" His voice reached out to her. "I have no wish to harm you. I am much moved by what you said. Did you say—" He faltered. "Did you say truly, you were glad of me here?"

She kept her face away from his. "I won't say it again. But I did say it. And it was true."

"Then let's do all this gently, Nan," he beseeched, "for old times' sake. I have to prove that I can father a king to follow me. That was why I left Katherine, why

I turned to you. It's why I must leave you now and turn to someone else, but it can be done all simply and gently, without this Court or the headsman."

"How?" she asked, almost hoping.

"If I'm to marry again you must somehow free me. Divorce won't do, because that would leave Elizabeth the heir."

"Why must you leave a king to follow you, Henry? Why not a queen?"

"This country's never been ruled by a queen. I doubt that it could be. You and I, we'll not have a son now. God has spoken there. I must have my king's sons elsewhere. And it grows late; I'm not as young as I was."

"And what do you want of me?"

"Go quietly," he said. "Sign a nullification of our marriage. Live abroad with Elizabeth. You'd be cared for. Leave me free."

She looked steadily at him for a moment. Then she shook her head. "No," she said. "Once we danced together, and I told you any children we had would be bastards. You promised me to change that. Now you dance out of your promise and reduce to bastards again. Well, I won't do it. We were King and Queen, man and wife together. I keep that. Take it from me as best you can."

"Anne," he warned. "You leave me no choice!"

"You've already made the choice," she said with a rueful smile. "What you truly want is a fresh frail innocent maid who'll make you feel fresh and innocent again." Her voice beat against him. "Jane Seymour is the name! It could be anyone, only let her be virginal and sweet. And when you've had her you'll want someone else."

"It's not true."

"Meanwhile, to get her, you'll murder if you must!"

The angry blood rose to his cheeks. "Why, then you've decided. And so have I!"

He started back toward the door.

"Before you go," she flashed out at him, "perhaps you should hear one thing. I lied to you. I loved you, but I lied to you. I was untrue. Untrue with many!"

"This is a lie!"

"Is it? Take it to your grave. I was unfaithful to you with all of them, with half your court. Look for the rest of your life at every man that ever knew me and wonder if I didn't find him a better man than you!"

He cried out, "You whore!" and struck her with his hand across the face.

She pressed her fingers to her reddened cheek, but she smiled.

"But Elizabeth was yours," she told him. "Watch her as she grows. She's yours, she's a Tudor! Get yourself a son on that pale Seymour girl if you can, and hope that it will live, but Elizabeth shall reign after you: Elizabeth, the child of Anne, the whore, and Henry, the blood-stained lecher!"

"Why, then, it's settled," he raged back. "You asked for death, you shall have it."

"So be it," she replied. "What I take to my grave, you take to yours." Her voice rose as she confronted him. "And think of this: Elizabeth shall be a greater queen than any king of yours. She shall rule a greater England than any you could ever have built. My Elizabeth shall be Queen, and my blood will have been well spent!"

Henry turned and went storming through the door.

Anne heard it clang behind her. She was alone in the cell. The sound of the hammers, still at their work, came from the Tower Green.

Anne listened, not daring to let her defiance give way to tears.

But they came.

"I wonder," she said aloud, weeping to the walls of her empty cell, "what will become of my little girl when she must go on alone?"

Fifty-One

Henry sat bleary-eyed, in his room at dawn. Cromwell stood by him. The warrant for Anne's execution lay between them on the table.

"May I have your signature, Sire?" Cromwell said.

Anne's face still lingered in the King's mind. Her voice still rang in his ears.

"She lies," he muttered, burying his face in his hands. "She lies. She was not unfaithful to me. And yet—if she were— She could. Any woman could—And yet she lies!" He raised his head. "If she lies, let her die for lying! Let her die!"

He took the pen from Cromwell's hand and signed the warrant.

Fifty-Two

The trestle scaffold was ready on Tower Green. Two men were strewing rushes over the platform while the executioner and his assistant, brought especially from France, were testing the sword.

Below the scaffold, guards stolidly waited in the bright spring sunlight. Now the big cannon was being loaded, and drummers were marching to position themselves near the scaffold.

The time was drawing near.

Norfolk and Boleyn appeared with three other peers who had served with them as Anne's judges. They walked to the door of the Tower chapel, where Sir William Kingston stood waiting.

"Is everything ready?" Norfolk asked.

"Yes, my lord. The Queen is at prayer."

"Fetch her," said Norfolk. "The time for prayer is past."

Kingston nodded and went into the chapel.

"And where is the King?" inquired Boleyn.

"At Richmond," Norfolk answered. "There is a hunt today."

"Will you join him later?"

Norfolk glanced grimly at his brother-in-law, at the man who had been perhaps the most cold-blooded self-seeker of all the self-seekers at the court. "No, by God," he answered curtly. "For me there is killing enough today."

Inside the chapel, Anne knelt in prayer. Three ladies-in-waiting, dressed in deepest black, knelt in a row behind her.

Kingston stood inside the door.

He waited until Anne crossed herself and rose to her feet. Then he moved to her.

She hesitated. Then, "Will it hurt?" she asked.

Kingston glanced down at his feet. "They say not, Madam. The executioner from France is an expert with the sword."

She laughed. "I hear that he is good, and I have such a little neck." She laughed again. Then suddenly she lowered her head and sobbed.

"Oh, Madam!" Kingston cried.

He raised his hands in a futile gesture of comfort and protection. But Anne had already recovered.

"No, Kingston, no. Come. I am glad to die."

The sunlight beyond the door struck at her like a blow. Her eyes beheld the scaffold, and nearby a slender tree in bloom: a May tree.

"The month is May!" she cried.

"Madam?" Kingston said.

"Nothing."

Norfolk and Boleyn and the other peers walked slowly toward the scaffold. Anne did not turn her head toward them. Step by step she approached the platform, her eyes fixed on the headsman. His face was covered by a black mask. His chest bore two initials: H.R.

She reached the foot of the scaffold and began to ascend. A clock from the Tower began striking the hour of noon.

The drums rolled. She moved toward the block. She knelt and committed her soul to God.

The cannon fired. The officer of the guard raised his sword in signal.

The headsman in turn raised his sword high over his head.

For an instant, Anne raised her eyes.

The headsman muttered to his assistant in French, "She looks at me. Distract her!"

The assistant moved before Anne. She turned her head to look.

The executioner brought down his sword.

Cannon fire filled the air.

It was over. The Queen was dead.

Fifty-Three

Henry, hunting with his party in Richmond Park, heard the distant cannons.

He shuddered.

Then he turned and looked at his apprehensive companions. There was no expression on his face.

He called suddenly, "Away, my lords!"

"Where to, Your Grace" the nearest courtier called back.

Henry wheeled his horse and rode at full gallop down the green slope.

"To Mistress Seymour's!"

The others galloped after him.

Fifty-Four

In the gardens of Greenwich a little girl with fiery red hair was walking. She was alone, and she moved with stiff solemn steps because she was wearing a train, but this was not merely a game she was playing. She knew she was a princess of England, who might one day be Queen.

Suddenly, through the peaceful air came the sound of cannon fire. The child stopped and looked up, listening.

After a while the rumbling died away.

Then, looking straight ahead of her, she walked toward the palace.

ANNE BOLEYN'S LAST LETTER TO KING HENRY

SIR:

Your grace's displeasure, and my imprisonment, are things so strange unto me, as what to write, or what to excuse, I am altogether ignorant. Whereas you send unto me, willing me to confess a truth (and so obtain your favor) by such an one as you know to be mine ancient professed enemy, I no sooner received this message by him than I rightly conceived your meaning, and if, as you say, confessing a truth indeed may procure my safety, I shall with all willingness and duty perform your command.

But let not your grace ever imagine that your poor wife will ever be brought to acknowledge a fault, where not so much as a thought thereof proceeded. And to speak a truth, never prince had wife more loyal in all duty, and in all true affection, than you have ever found of Anne Boleyn, with which name and place I could willingly have contented myself, if God and your grace's pleasure had been so pleased. Neither did I at any time so far forget myself in my exaltation, or received queenship, but that I always looked for such an alteration as now I find: for the ground of my preferment being on no surer foundation than your grace's fancy, the least alteration I knew was fit and sufficient to draw that fancy to some other subject. You have chosen me from a low estate to be your queen and companion, far beyond my desert or desire. If then you found me worthy of such honour,

good your grace let not any light fancy nor bad counsel of mine enemies, withdraw your princely favour
from me; neither let that stain, that unworthy stain, of
a disloyal heart towards your good grace, ever cast a
blot on your most dutiful wife, and the infant princess, your daughter; try me, good king, but let me
have a lawful trial, and let not my sworn enemies sit
as my accusers and judges: yea, let me receive an
open trial, for my truth shall fear no open shame:
then shall you see, either mine innocence cleared,
your suspicion and conscience satisfied, the ignominy
and slander of the world stopped, or my guilt openly
declared. So that, whatsoever God and you may de-
termine of me, your grace may be freed from an open
censure; and mine offence, being so lawfully proved,
your grace is at liberty, both before God and man,
not only to execute worthy punishment on me as an
unlawful wife, but to follow your affection already
settled on that party, for whose sake I am now as I
am, whose name some good while since I could have
pointed unto: your grace not being ignorant of my
suspicion therein.

But, if you have already determined of me, and
that only my death, but an infamous slander must
bring you the enjoying of your desired happiness:
then I desire of God, that he will pardon your great
sin therein, and that he will not call you to a strict account for your unprincely and cruel usage of me, at
his general judgment-seat, where both you and myself
must shortly appear; and in whose judgment, I doubt
not (whatsoever the world may think of me) mine innocence shall be openly known, and sufficiently
cleared.

My last and only request shall be, that myself may
only bear the burthen of your grace's displeasure, and
that it may not touch the innocent souls of those poor
gentlemen who, as I understand, are likewise in strait
imprisonment for my sake. If ever I have found favour in your sight, if ever the name of Anne Boleyn
hath been pleasing in your ears, then let me obtain this
request, and I will so leave to trouble your grace any
further; with mine earnest prayers to the Trinity to have

your good grace in his keeping, and to direct you in all your actions. From my doleful prison in the Tower, this sixth of May.

Your most loyal and ever faithful wife
ANNE BOLEYN